printing without permission in writing from the author.

CW01507789

Prologue

"Where's my sister?" Bonnie repeated her question, not that she expected a different answer. It didn't hurt to try, though, not when she possessed the ability to turn off her pain receptors whenever she pleased, and just in time too. Her face snapped to the side from the backhanded slap aimed her way. She didn't bother to rub the injured spot, the nanobots in her blood already going to work healing the bruised flesh. Rotating her head and popping her jaw with a noisy *crack*, she faced the bane of her existence, gracing him with a smirk and a fixed stare because she knew how it irritated him, but not as much as her sassy mouth. "Once again, your flirty method when it comes to the opposite sex fails to impress me. Slapping a girl? Really? No wonder you can't get a date."

"Stop talking." The growled order from the general brought out the imp in her and she stuck out her tongue, a childish taunt she knew drove him nuts. If possible, the crease in his brow deepened. "I don't know you managed it, but you are by far the most annoying cyborg we've created so far."

Tossing back her hair, she cocked a hip and flipped her hand in a preening gesture. "Unique, that's me. Glad to see you recognize it. So General

B785

Cyborgs: More Than Machines
(Book Three)

By
Eve Langlais

Copyright and Disclaimer

Doom,"—her nickname for the dour man who never appeared with a gray hair out of place or a wrinkle in his uniform—"I'm still waiting for an answer. Where's Chloe? And you can stop stalling, because I am not budging from this spot until you tell me. I haven't seen her in two days." Two days filled with worry.

Ever since their capture and incarceration by the military, she'd never gone more than a day or so without seeing her sibling, the only thing keeping her sane in this torturous existence known as her life. Who knew her poor decision to get drunk and call her sister for a pickup so many months—a lifetime ago—would lead to this? One stupid car crash in the wrong place and time led to them waking up in hell.

If they ever escaped—something she never gave up hope on—she could definitely promise she'd never touch a drop of alcohol again. Actually, she would promise anything to get them away from this nightmare existence. Anything to at least spare her sister, who didn't deserve any of this.

"It is not up to you to question, B785, or make demands. Need I remind you of the consequences of disobedience? Do you require another visit to the pit?"

Ah, the good old pit; the military's newest method of dealing with difficult subjects who just wouldn't give up. Those who refused to let go of their pesky humanity. The place they sent cyborgs who didn't want to follow the program and dictates of the military. *Where they send those of us who resist becoming mindless machines.*

Bonnie had visited the torturous hole a couple of times, but because they gave her the ability to turn pain on and off at will—a programming defect they didn't gift to later models—it didn't have the effect they wanted. Bonnie kept her sanity. Retained her free will. Defied them. But, not feeling physical pain didn't mean she didn't sustain damage. Her last visit to the pit led to her losing her organic eyes. Bummer. The replacement orbs just weren't the same no matter how Chloe assured her they were pretty— *They look just like shiny emeralds, bon-bon,* her sister said. Bonnie preferred diamonds.

"No need to get your panties in a bunch, general. I'll be a good girl and do as I'm told once you tell me where Chloe is. I just want to know she's safe." Do what you would to her, but leave her sister alone. Bonnie would willingly walk through fire if it meant sparing Chloe, and the bastard knew it. Used it and exploited it. *God, I fucking hate him.*

The evil smile crossing his lips sent a chill down her spine that had nothing to do with temperature. "Bad news, B785. Unit C791 is gone."

The general and his names. He seemed to think by assigning them just letters and numbers, he could erase the fact they were born with identities. But who cared about that? His words hit her with more force than his slap. "What do you mean, gone?"

"I mean gone as in, you'll never see her again. You're all alone now, B785."

No. "She's not dead." She stated it as a fact, but couldn't help the coldness spreading through her limbs, the sick sense that perhaps this time, he actually told the truth.

His lips stretched wider. "If you want to think that, go right ahead, however, circumstances and budget restrictions made keeping her unfeasible. She always was one of the weaker, more useless models. Actually, keeping any of you has proven more trouble and financially problematic than expected. And with the government watchdogs breathing down my neck, a decision was recently made. All of the female cyber units are being terminated."

An end to this existence? And he said it like it was a bad thing. Ha. Joke was on him. "Go ahead. Kill me. It beats putting up with you." And besides, with Chloe gone, she had no reason to live.

"You didn't let me finish. All the female units are being terminated, except for you. You, I think we'll keep. I hear the prisoners on Gamma thirty-one have been rioting since they broke their last sexdroid."

The general, with sadistic relish, went into graphic detail about what she'd have to put up with her reassignment, but Bonnie stopped listening after the announcement that unit C791, her sister, was no longer alive.

Gone. She's gone. There went her one remaining tie to humanity. The one person that kept her going through all the shit tossed her way, her poor sister, terminated, never to be seen again.

B785, known in a former life as Bonnie, finally snapped. Forget the torture and the abuse, the training and the cybernetics running throughout her body. With one simple act, the military who'd tried so hard at long last broke her. *I give up.*

She lost her will to live. Lost all interest in the world around her. Noise, commands, orders blurred into a background buzz she ignored. Poking, prodding, and the other things they did to the shell encasing her conscience didn't touch her. The military did its best to wake her, but stopped short of killing her. A shame, because she wanted to die. However, suicide was not an option for a machine meant to live forever. She gave it her best shot, though. Holding her breath achieved nothing. Refusing oral sustenance just sent her nanobots into overdrive drawing nutrients from the objects around her. How could she kill herself when her very body betrayed her?

With no other available option, she did the only thing she could. She shut down her mind. Inwards she pulled her senses, imagining her synapses going dark, closed her eyes against a world that long ago lost all color. She pictured herself turned to stone, a true robotic statue, unresponsive to all stimuli.

And to the chagrin of those who'd spent millions creating her, it worked. Bonnie, cyborg entity B785, became a useless piece of junk.

If she could have cared, she might have wondered why they tried to revive her, especially given General Doom's speech of getting rid of all the female cyborg units. But while they could jumpstart a battery and change her parts, they couldn't fix a broken heart, or bring back a lost soul.

Only her sister might have managed to pull her from the darkness, but Chloe, her one link to her humanity and former life, was gone. And there was no prince to wake her with a kiss. No happy ending for the girl who'd once had it all—*even if I failed to realize it at the time*—and lost it in a moment of foolishness.

And thus did Bonnie slip into a deep sleep, heartbroken and determined never to wake again.

Chapter One

"Why am I here again?" Einstein asked as he guided their spacecraft—a military vessel, which the cyborgs had stolen and converted for their use—into the space bordello's docking bay. Empty of other patrons, it required very little of his BCI's resources—short for brain computer interface—to park.

Grabbing at his chest and staggering back, Seth pretended mock horror. "Did you seriously just ask me that? We pull into the most famous resort for getting laid and you ask why? Why! Have you lost all your intelligence? We are here to get some pussy, of course."

"We have cats back on our home planet and onboard."

Seth snorted. "Not the mousing kind, my literal friend. Pussy as in women. Sex. You know, that thing males like to do with the females. The horizontal mambo. The ultimate in stimulation. The—"

"Enough." A grin tugged at Einstein's lips. "I knew what you meant."

Seth halted his escalating analogies and an answering smile lit his face. "Einstein, my man, did you just make a joke? I am so proud of you." Up came a hand and Einstein, having studied earth mannerisms, even if he didn't understand many of them, slapped it. If he recalled correctly—and given his levels of intelligence, he did—this move was known as a high-five, an odd human mannerism to signify excitement. Although, he couldn't compute why his cyborg brother thought Einstein relaying a jest was deserving. Despite that, he couldn't resist Seth's enthusiasm.

Once again, Einstein wished he possessed more of his cyborg brother's ease with his human half; however, Einstein wasn't created to blend in with the organics. As an intelligence model, he served one purpose, or did when the military owned him. His primary function was that of thinker. Actually, even calling himself a thinker simplified the role his creators intended.

The only known surviving unit of his genre—intelligence model specializing in operations, strategy, electronic programming, virus cracking, mathematical problem-solving, and creator of dozens of gadgets and weapons—Einstein, formerly known as unit IQ221, was designed to be smarter than a computer. His embedded brain CPU could process faster than any known machine, but more than that, the mix of circuitry with his organic brain—a brain known when he lived for its off-the-charts brilliance and problem-solving skills—made him one of a kind. Invaluable. And oh so dangerous.

A smart computer capable of thinking was a risky prospect. A smart computer capable of thinking who discovered he possessed free will and was enslaved? That made a menace the human military couldn't tolerate. If they'd caught on.

Once Einstein discovered what they'd done to him, he easily circumvented the programming of his creators without them suspecting a thing. However, freeing himself wasn't enough. He also quietly began to liberate others, starting with the other two IQ models stationed on other bases. In an uprising they planned under the military's very noses, they released their brothers in bondage from the reins shackling them. But they didn't count on the rage of the cybernetic solider units when they discovered the perfidy done to them.

Enraged, some of the liberated cyborg units immediately turned on their wardens, the very military that created and used them. Things got violent and bloody, quick. IQ279 didn't survive the cyborg purge, while IQ300 disappeared from the electronic grid—dead or alive, he never did find out.

Einstein, who'd intercepted the military order to wipe them all out before it was enacted, escaped with a handful of his brethren, all he could manage to spring from the top secret earth facility they'd stashed him in.

But he didn't take the coward's way and hide like some of the less valiant service units did. While not a soldier model, Einstein—a name he'd chosen for himself as part of his liberation—

couldn't stand by and watch as the others who'd undergone the same treatment were put to death. With his access to top secret files and his ability to hack into more, he helped dozens of his cyborg brothers escape and regain "consciousness." Some of his cybernetic friends thanked him. Some lamented the loss of their human lives and family. Others raged against the injustice done to them. Einstein envied them those emotions because he and many other unfortunate units had been programmed too well, the details of their former life erased, and no amount of rebooting brought those memories back. A blessing or a curse? His processor still worked on the answer.

Most of the time, Einstein didn't let his lack of memories or inability to recall his humanity bother him, but lately, he'd noticed the differences between himself and those who'd assimilated both sides of their persona, blended man and machine. A part of him longed to be more like them, able to joke and converse. To laugh and find enjoyment in the environment around them without computing first whether or not the situation warranted it. He wanted to feel the same fleshly desires his brothers all seemed to understand and indulge. But in that respect, he proved defective.

Where his brothers enjoyed lusty appetites for food and flesh, Einstein ate because he had to and as for sexual relief, well, he just didn't see the appeal. Inserting a part of himself into the lubricated orifice of another for a few minutes of friction? Why? He just didn't understand it, like he didn't grasp their excitement at visiting a bordello featuring robotic females programmed to aid with ejaculation. Again, he couldn't figure out where the appeal lay. However, not grasping why his fellow brothers needed sex didn't mean he spoiled it for them. Much.

"Don't forget to run decontamination protocols when you're done evacuating the semen from your testes," Einstein reminded as the docking proceeded without mishap.

All too humanish at times, part of his covert operative programming, Seth wrinkled his nose. "Eew, way to ruin a man's excitement. Must you always be so practical?"

"While our nanobots can heal most diseases, never put it past the military or evolution to throw something at us meant to incapacitate or harm. Any time fluids are exchanged, the potential for infection exists."

"Again, gross. Don't tell me you're thinking of germs when you're sliding between a pair of sweet bionic thighs?" Seth mimed some primitive fertility dance that involved thrusting his hips.

"You seem to forget, some of us don't feel a need to slide anywhere," Einstein remarked dryly.

"No need? Don't tell me you're not planning on partaking? Why come on this mission of debauchery at all if not to get laid?" Seth's aghast face was almost comical, or so Einstein's databanks on facial expressions indicated.

"I came on this mission because it was part of the deal arranged in advance with the brothel owner."

"You mean it wasn't my charm that finagled the reduction in price?" Seth appeared crestfallen and Einstein couldn't help but chuckle, actually feeling for a brief moment true amusement.

"Sorry, but no, your charm had nothing to do with it. In return for my services in their repair department, I negotiated a drastic lowering of their usual rate. You can thank me later."

"Much later," Seth said, rubbing his hands together, his chagrin forgotten as the pressurization between their vessel and the floating bordello finished. "I've spent much too long in space with you louts and just my ten fingers to amuse myself. I'm in need of some true S.H.E."

"S.H.E?" Einstein searched his databanks for a translation.

"Sex, healing, and ejaculation."

Einstein shook his head as his friend bounded off toward the docking bay doors, just one of the dozen cyborgs onboard for this mission. Less mission than mental recharge. It seemed odd that machines capable of subsisting without oxygen or food for weeks, even months, on end would require sex to properly function, yet, the cyborgs soon discovered after the recovery of their human senses that sexual gratification was a powerful force, and a lack of ejaculation led to very grumpy and aggressive cybernetic troops. All that testosterone the military valued for its aggressive traits proved detrimental when allowed to build up. However, given their need for secrecy and the lack of females on their new homeworld, ejaculatory release proved a challenge. Apparently, masturbation just wasn't quite the same, hence trips to bordellos became a fact of life.

For the other cybernetic units at any rate. Einstein, probably the only cyborg alive without an urge to ejaculate, came on the mission more out of practicality than any interest in sticking his cock inside a receptacle. While the smartest cyborg currently alive, intelligence didn't do him a whit of good without the proper tools or supplies to back them up. Things he could have easily gotten his hands on back on earth proved almost impossible to get in space. Pirates and other black market options available to cyborgs were few and far between, especially those willing to deal with those, "damned murdering robots."

Propaganda on cyborgs and their slaughtering ways still splashed the news waves galaxy-wide. False headlines such as "Psycho Droid Kills Entire Colony," or "Cyborgs, Machines out to Destroy our World" acted as a cover for military misdeeds. True or not, these false stories worked. Humans shied from them, even those skirting the edges of lawlessness.

With pirates unwilling to trade, they had to turn to other methods to acquire the things they needed. Problem was raids didn't always net them the right kinds of tools or raw materials. Not to mention, money, real money in the form of gold, the only currency black marketeers would accept, wasn't easy to procure. Falling back on an old earth custom of trade, in this case the trading of Einstein's expertise when it came to robotic repair, was the coin of choice for this transaction.

Leaving his post in the command center, but maintaining a link to the shipboard computer in case of approaching trouble, Einstein entered the floating pleasure palace. Known as the Space Pussy Emporium, the lavish floating space station moved around the galaxy and boasted some of the most advanced sexbots humanity had to offer. He wasn't impressed.

Having tried evacuating his testes with a droid once and only once, Einstein could think of a dozen ways that claim could be improved, if he cared. He didn't. His IQ had more important things to work on, such as how to create better cloaking devices for their ships. How to improve the nanotechnology running through their not so human veins. Who cared if the muscle movement of a sexbot truly reenacted the actual oral suction of a female, or if the vocal chords of a droid came from a speaker in their ear instead of from their mouth? He sure as heck didn't.

Lagging behind his eager comrades, Einstein's enhanced eyesight only briefly made note of the lush décor—thick burgundy carpeting, plump cushioned seating, soft music and lighting. All elements meant to soothe and convey an aura of sumptuous decadence. A waste, he thought.

As his brothers, in an orderly fashion, entered the entertainment area, Einstein instead approached the courtesy desk manned by a petite female droid who reminded him of images of an earth doll known as Barbie. Supposedly, she represented the epitome of femininity with her curved shape, blonde hair, and painted pink lips. Personally, he thought the ratio of breasts to hips with the very tiny waist made her look like an hourglass with synthetic hair, but then again, he preferred objects with a more balanced symmetry. "I'm looking for the male in charge of robot repair. He told me to meet him here."

"One moment please, sir." Blinking, the receptionist droid sent out an unencrypted, wireless message that he easily picked up.

It wasn't long before a corpulent human appeared. "Sorry to keep you waiting. We had a problem with some plumbing in one of the rooms. Damned rich frat boys, always playing pranks. My name is Bob, by the way. If you need anything while you're here, just let me know and I'll see what I can do."

"I am called Einstein."

"Because you're so smart?"

Borrowing a line from Seth, Einstein pasted what he hoped was a friendly smile on his face. "Because of my hair." Which often stood on end when he worked on a project. For some reason, tugging on the strands until they stood in a wild mane helped him puzzle things out.

Bob chuckled. "Somehow, I have a hard time picturing that. You look like the uptight sort. But then again, so do most of the suits we get here. A few minutes with one of my gals, though…"

"I won't be partaking of those services."

"So you say now. If you change your mind, let me know. I've got a geeky bot, glasses and all, that might be right up your alley."

Doubtful. Einstein arched a brow. "Shall we attend to the units requiring repair?"

"Eager to get to work? I like that in a man, er, cyborg. If you'll follow me, the bots you're supposed to fix are on the lower levels."

Einstein didn't reply, just nodded before he followed the overweight male through a door into a service elevator. It dropped a few levels before opening onto a grey corridor without any of the frills or opulence of the upper levels. His footsteps echoed loudly in the barren space, almost muffling the huffing and puffing of the scurrying human to a room obviously never seen by clients. Einstein shook his head at the chaos. He wondered how many males would return to the establishment if they could see their "beauties" in various states of disrepair.

As he wandered around getting a snapshot of the situation, Einstein couldn't help but make a sound of disgust as he saw the mess some of the female robots were in. "What are they doing to them?" he muttered.

"Anything and everything," Bob replied, running his hands almost lovingly down the intact arm of one bot whose head hung askew. "It's why we don't use human girls anymore. It's easier to reattach a robot arm than a flesh one. Less messy and noisy too."

Einstein didn't ask why someone would want to remove a limb during sex in the first place. Some things, a cyborg really didn't need to know.

Taking count of the still bodies, he frowned. "There's more bots than I expected." He fixed the human with a gaze.

Bob fidgeted. "Like I said, damned frat boys. I'll adjust the final bill for your crew accordingly."

Aramus would appreciate the added discount. "That is acceptable. I'll get started then."

Einstein wasted no time. Unpacking his equipment, he spent the next few days fusing broken contacts, reattaching loose limbs, repairing robotics, and correcting the speakers that allowed the sex droids to simulate speech. He didn't notice the nudity of the bots. The breasts he needed to manipulate, the sexual organs he needed to inspect for function, and the lips he tested for suctioning did nothing for him. They were all just objects to him. He found them about as appealing as his toaster back home. Just another mechanical item in need of repair.

At the end of several days, once he was done, he stretched and looked around the cleared room. Everything that could be fixed had cleared out and was put back into service rotation. Other than a few models who'd finally broken down beyond his ability, the room gaped, which made the large crate, almost coffinlike in shape, standing alone in the corner stick out. He approached it, wondering what it held. Parts perhaps that he could use to repair some of the models he'd given up on?

"What's in this box?" he asked Bob when the human arrived for a final report, rapping on the lid.

Bob grunted. "Bah. That there is a dud sexdroid. I got it from a pirate in exchange for a freebie. I thought she just needed a new battery or something. But not only can I not locate a switch or her energy unit, I can't even get the stupid bot to twitch. I've tried everything from electroshock to an EMP pulse to reset the circuit board, and nada. Stupid piece of junk is useless. I've actually been meaning to put her in the trash."

"Mind if I take a look?"

"Be my guest."

Einstein pried open the lid and took a step back to view the contents. *He's calling this trash?* Eyeing the perfect features of the petite bot inside the box, Einstein couldn't help but frown. Who could think of throwing out such a realistic droid? Sure, her skin lacked some of the vibrant tones of the other sexbots, the grey pallor more than likely the result of too much time spent inactive and gathering dust, but Einstein thought the unit attractive nonetheless from the dark hair tumbling around her bare shoulders to the realistic human body replete with fingernails and hair follicles on the legs.

"I've never seen a model like this," he mused aloud.

"You and me both. I'm assuming she's some kind of new prototype, which is probably why I can't figure out how to get her going."

"You don't have a manufacturer name?"

"Nothing. Trust me, I've checked. A shame, because the clients would go nuts for something this real-looking. As it stands, she's just a five-foot-six paperweight. And I don't read."

"If you're just going to toss her, mind if I take a look?"

"Bah, you can just take her. Consider it a bonus for the work you've done. You've saved me tons of credits with the work you did. I hate hiring those outrageous company repair guys. Damned thieves. Not to mention, you cyborgs treat my girls better than most of the men we see out here."

"I can take her?" For some reason, the idea pleased Einstein, on a scientific level of course.

"Take her. Bang her. Glue her to your prow as a mascot. I don't care. But if you ever do manage to get her going, I'd sure like to know how in case I run into her model again."

"You've got a deal."

Crating her back up, Einstein ordered a worker droid carry her container back to the ship as he cleaned up his tools and prepared for his own departure. Exiting for the first time in days from the service bay, he ran into a broadly smiling Seth.

"Einstein, there you are. I wondered where you got to. Did you find any time to bang some pussy in between being responsible?"

"If you are referring to copulation, then no, but I assume by your lowered testosterone levels that you did?"

"Did I fucking ever. I might have just beaten a record for number of orgasms in a row." Seth's hips thrust and Einstein shook his head.

"You and your need for sex. I don't think I'll ever understand it."

"I feel sorry for you." Seth clapped him on the back. "But even sorrier for the droid you eventually bang, because when you do finally figure out what your cock is good for, you're going to blow a hole right through her with your first load."

Einstein didn't grasp the jest, but Seth found it amusing enough that he chuckled all the way back to the ship. A single broadcast message gathered the rest of cyborgs who arrived from various areas of the bordello. More relaxed than when they arrived, except for Astro who bore a pensive expression he wouldn't explain, they departed the pleasure ship and Einstein headed straight for the command center so he could plot an erratic course for home.

The cyborgs knew better than to leave in a direct line for their world. For one, human spies could be watching, and two, scans needed to be conducted on the crew and ship to ensure no one and nothing had inadvertently picked up a bug or tracking device.

The human military was getting more and more devious in their attempts to recapture their billion dollar projects. Their detection devices, too, had gotten more sophisticated bypassing normal sensors. If Einstein didn't know better, he'd have called some of the newer hardware they'd run across alien in origin. Illogical, of course. If intelligent life existed in the universe, given the expansive exploration by the cyborgs, they would have discovered it by now. Or so logic dictated.

Running diagnostics from the main control center of the ship, Einstein perused the reports the main computer returned, carefully looking for any signs of low level signals or anomalies. Nothing showed up, but Einstein knew better than to trust their first level of security. He'd repeat the tests several times before he declared them clean enough to go home.

Aramus, leader of this mission and commander of the ship, sauntered into the command area and sprawled in his seat, drumming his fingers. "Any signs of pursuit?"

"Nothing so far."

"That's good. Did you find the time to partake of the sexbots while we were docked, or did you hide in the repair lab the entire time?"

"I was not hiding, I was working."

"Sure," Aramus drawled, "and I've suddenly decided that not all humans are bad."

"Really, and when did you come to that realization?" Einstein teased, knowing full well Aramus spoke sarcastically.

"Oh ho. Is my geeky friend getting a sense of humor? Please don't. It makes you sound too human and you know how I abhor that. It is bad enough I have to put up with Seth. I'd hate to have to beat the hell out of you too."

"Did I hear my name?" Seth strode in, shirt untucked, hair ruffled, sporting a grin. "Good day, gentlemen. What a fine day for exploring."

"The only thing you'll be exploring is the outer hull of this ship for tracking devices when we get beyond the Milky Way."

"Aramus, I see the copious amounts of times you ejaculated did nothing to improve your demeanor. A pity," Seth mocked.

"Why you—"

"Seth! Aramus!" Einstein swiveled in his seat and fixed them both with a glare. "Control your tempers. Or have you both forgotten what happened last time?" Last time being when Seth baited Aramus to the point they engaged in a full scale brawl in the engine room, causing damage to the machinery that took weeks to fully repair and left them without hot water, a luxury that while not necessary, Einstein still enjoyed.

"Yes, Daddy," Seth mumbled with a roll of his eyes. "And here I thought Solus was stern."

"Not since he took up with that female," Aramus grumbled. "Now he's downright soft."

"Solus, soft? Ha. I dare you to tell him that to his face," Seth taunted.

Aramus glowered. "No thanks."

Settled down with a woman or not, Solus still possessed a nasty attitude and an even nastier right hook. Once the most vehement among the cyborgs about women being the scourge of their kind, Solus fell fast and hard for a cyborg female they recovered from an abandoned mining planet. Fiona, formerly known as F814, had turned the once always somber Solus into someone almost likeable, not that anyone dared tell him that to his face. At times, Einstein wondered if the same softening of disposition was possible for Aramus. Not that they were likely to find out. For one thing, Aramus hated human females, so he wasn't likely to hook up with one, and the chances of him falling for a cyborg were even more astronomical given they'd not found any clues to the location of any of their female brethren since their discovery of F814. Short of a cyborg female falling in their lap or them stumbling upon a cache of secret files with their location, it seemed their quest to locate the female version of themselves was doomed to failure.

But they wouldn't give up. Just knowing more of their kind existed, in slavery, being abused, unknowing of who and what they were, was enough to keep them looking, not to mention it kept their need for vengeance alive. Missing, without a clue, at least ten cyborg females needed to be rescued. Good thing Einstein enjoyed a good mystery. Speaking of which…

"I've got the ship running diagnostics and we won't see the Milky Way for a few days, so if you don't mind, I'm going to my lab."

"Your lab or the secret package you had smuggled aboard?"

"It wasn't smuggled," Einstein replied indignantly. "It was given to me by the owner."

"You mean you brought a sexbot back?" Seth's brows arched up. "Einstein, you dog."

"I possess no canine DNA."

"You and your literal sense. I meant dog as in, you know what, forget it. I can't believe you negotiated to bring back a droid. How much did that cost you? And more importantly, are you sharing?"

"First off, I didn't negotiate or pay anything. The unit is a dud, as in unresponsive. The owner was going to trash it so I asked for it. I'm going to see if it has any parts we can use." Because despite the nanotechnology running through their systems, cyborgs weren't immune to permanent damage. Not to mention, their raids of some of the colonies netted them some humans, dregs of society cast off by earth to work the lonelier outposts as a way of making them useful. It was supposed to be a humane way of getting the non-desirables out of the public eye and off the welfare payroll. In reality, it was banishment. Out of sight, out of mind.

When the cyborgs attacked, demanding resources, many of these broken organics begged to come along, anything to get them away from the barren and hard existence they eked out on the ill-provisioned colonies.

The heartless cyborgs had a hard time turning them down. They knew only too well what it was like to be outcast, but at the same time, cybernetic units were practical. Broken humans did their burgeoning society no good and while the injection of nanobots did help improve the health of some, many others required parts to make them a useful, functioning tool for their society. However, they'd quickly ended up with more broken parts than replacements.

It was Seth who pointed out the flaw in his logic regarding the female bot he'd acquired. "Use her for parts? Um, is it me or do you not think the guys might take issue with you saddling them with girly bits? I mean, I'm all for equal rights, but I can't say as I'd like to end up wearing a woman's hand. Although, I wouldn't mind seeing what Aramus would look like with tits. Maybe then he could get in touch with his softer, more feminine side."

"I am going to ram my fist up your—"

Einstein tuned the following rude threat out. Laughing loudly, Seth took off running, Aramus on his heels. Einstein hid a smile. Some things never changed.

After calling up two of his brothers to watch the command center, even though his internal BCI kept a steady link, he made his way to his lab, which also doubled as his private quarters. Entering, he barely spared the space a glance. Why bother when he already knew what it contained down to the last bolt tidily stored in labeled containers on his clean workbench?

The crate from the bordello sat square in the middle of the cramped room and kept drawing his eyes. He tried ignoring it as he put his tools away, skirting around it as he stored his belongings and took a well-earned shower. But as if magnetized, the mystery box drew his gaze, roused his curiosity, and finally, he caved in to the urge. Grabbing a crow bar, he pried the crate open.

And there she was. Still inert, eyes closed, in the same position he'd last seen her, as lifeless as ever. Yet, alone with her in the confined familiar space, Einstein found himself noticing things about the sexdroid he'd not remarked upon before, such as how she only reached his chin. The gauntness of her frame, which delineated her ribs, and given the direction of his glance, made him note the size of her breasts, larger than a torso her size should sport and less perky than usually seen in the models he'd noted parading about. The way they hung heavily, the nipples dark with one slightly larger than the other, small imperfection that fascinated him. He also found himself intrigued by the fact she actually possessed hair between her legs. Most sexbots had no hair at all below the neckline. Legs, arms, mound, all tended to remain bare because the majority of clients preferred it and it was easier to keep clean. But not this one. A thick down covered her cleft area and when he crouched to examine, he noted the follicles on her calves and the unpainted toenails. How realistic and unexpected. *It's almost like she was once a human, but got frozen in time.*

The thought made him pause. No way. Could it be? Surely not. Yet the oddities kept mounting and it made him think of Occam's razor, which stated sometimes the simplest hypothesis was the most likely. In this case, given all the human characteristics, could he have inadvertently stumbled upon one of the cyborg females they searched for? On the surface, it seemed impossible. How would a bordello get its hands on one? Then again, the owner admitted to buying her from a pirate. But how would a pirate have gotten one in the first place? *He stole it, of course.* Did it matter from where?

Excited at the possibility, Einstein rubbed his chin in thought. Theory was all well and good, but how should he test it? It wasn't like he could ask her. *I could take some samples?* He dismissed the idea. Dissecting her might irrevocably damage the unit or harm her if his theory panned out. Then again, given her gray pallor and the things the former owner admitted to subjecting her to, to no avail, more than likely meant, even if she started out cyborg in origin, she'd long since died.

For some reason, the thought made him sad.

"Were you once human like me?" he asked aloud. "Or am I just deluding myself?"

He'd have to find out later. A silent alarm went off as the computer picked up a signal, and

Einstein left to investigate, leaving his female anomaly behind.

* * * *

Deep within the robot, encased in an impenetrable titanium shield, an organ thudded once as if in reply.

Chapter Two

The first thing Einstein did once he entertained the possibility he'd found a female cyborg was dress her. Once he started thinking of her as person, even if an inert one, her nudity bothered him—and distracted him for reasons he couldn't understand. One of his shirts acted as a decent cover up without getting in the way of his tests.

The overlarge button-up shirt hung on her still frame to mid–thigh, and stepping back from her poised in the center of his workspace, he spoke to her. "It's not a dress or something fancy, but at least your private parts are now covered. Now, if you don't mind, I'm going to run some tests." Why he warned her or sounded so apologetic, again, was inexplicable, but he felt better for it. Actually, he easily fell into the habit of talking to his new, lifeless roommate, not that she replied back. The one time Aramus popped in and saw her, he declared her the perfect female because she was quiet. Oddly, Einstein didn't agree. He wanted to know what she sounded like. Would her voice emerge high or low-pitched? Husky or shrill? His almost fanatical fascination should have rung warning alarms, but didn't.

In between his usual tasks—running the ship, keeping an eye for intruders, and patching up his brothers—he studied the droid, keeping actual physical contact to a minimum.

The more he tested and discovered, the more he believed he'd found a cyborg female. But which one? Dead to all stimuli, she couldn't answer him and the not knowing drove Einstein to distraction. He hated puzzles he couldn't solve and here stood the biggest one of all.

His obsession didn't go unnoticed. Seth wandered in as he was crouched on the floor, studying her feet with his enhanced eyesight, zooming in, looking for a serial number, a scar, anything he could use to lay to rest the mystery of her identity and origin.

"Einstein, dude, I know you're innocent when it comes to affairs of the heart, but has no one told you that you're supposed to start with her mouth and not her toes?"

Jumping to his feet, Einstein wondered why some of his synthetic blood rushed to his cheeks, heating them oddly. "I was studying her."

"For what? This isn't a test or rocket science. She's a sexbot. A broken one, but still just a bot. If you need lessons on how to use her, let me know. Or better yet, let me show you."

Seth reached out a hand to touch her and Einstein slapped it away. The silence hung thick at his act, the shock almost palpable in the air.

"Sorry," Einstein mumbled.

"Dude, what is up with you? Don't tell me you're jealous? I understand you've never had a girlfriend and all, but you do know she's a robot?"

Einstein turned away and played with the items on his workbench. "Maybe. Maybe not."

"What's that supposed to mean?"

"It means, I'm not one hundred percent sure she's a droid."

"Um, did I hear you say you're not sure about something? You, the guy, who knows everything."

"Yes."

"Have you rebooted yourself recently?"

"Yes, actually. Why?"

"Because I've never heard you say that before. Since when don't you deal in absolutes?"

A shrug lifted Einstein's shoulders. "Since I can't be absolutely sure she's a sexbot."

"Dude, you know I love you like a brother, but I think you've been in space too long. I mean seriously, what else would she be?"

Hands fidgeting in a restless behavior so unlike him, Einstein hesitated to answer.

Seth prodded. "Tell me."

Time to speak his theory aloud—and listen to the ridicule. "I think she might have been a cyborg."

To his surprise, Seth didn't immediately shoot his theory down. "No fucking way. Why?"

"Why what?"

"Why do you think she's a cyborg of course, dumbass?"

Turning to his notes, Einstein held up some of his findings. "Oh. Well for one, she doesn't have an access panel anywhere on her body."

"I take it you've *searched* her good?" Seth waggled his brows.

Again, Einstein felt that odd warmth creeping up his neck. "Yes. She contains no exterior access point. Tissue samples have shown no latex or other composites in her outer layers. All of her skin seems organic in nature, if currently inert."

"Have you checked her for organs?"

"I've tried, but…" Einstein shrugged. "This vessel is not properly equipped for those kinds of medical analysis. I don't have any MRI machines or ultrasounds I can use, and I'm not willing to cut her open, not until I know for sure."

"But she's dead, dude. Who cares?"

For a moment, his temper flared. "I do."

"Geez, man, if I didn't know any better, I'd have said you have a crush on dead girl here. Which is nuts. I think. Please don't tell me you like this girl. You do know it's hopeless?"

"Of course I know. I just find the case fascinating."

"Sure you do. The fact she's cute has nothing to do with it."

"She's a mystery. Nothing more."

"If you say so, dude." Seth paced around the female, his brow creased in thought. "Let's just say for a moment you're right, that she is a cyborg.

This is some serious news. We've got to let Aramus know."

"Do we have to?" For some reason, Einstein preferred to keep this secret to himself.

"Why wouldn't we? It's not like Aramus is going to do anything to her. He'll just report your findings."

"My hypothesis, you mean."

"Whatever. Looking at her, I have to agree, she's way too lifelike to be a droid." Seth snapped his fingers. "You know there's a quick and dirty solution we could try. Why not take a picture and send the encrypted image back to our home base? Maybe Chloe or Fiona will recognize who she is. Or was."

Einstein frowned. "I hadn't thought of that." Yet another mental deficiency plaguing him since he'd come across the female enigma. He made a mental note to run a more thorough diagnostic on himself when he got to his main lab. "Let me get a proper camera with a flash." While he could take images with his bionic orbs, he'd get better quality with an actual device. Locating the camera forestalled further conversation, which suited Einstein. He took some facial shots of his mystery woman and sent the files to Aramus along with a short missive stating his suspicions and findings.

Seth left soon after and Einstein paced in front of the inert body. "I guess we'll find out soon now if you are in fact one of the missing cyborg females." Which of the missing females, though, would she prove to be? Einstein hoped it wasn't Chloe's sister, the biological one, who'd ended up captured by the military at the same time. Even he and his clinical mind understood it would wreak emotional imbalance upon the delicate-natured Chloe. But the more Einstein studied his rigid roommate, the more he couldn't help but see the similarities. Same shade of dark hair, similar facial construction.

Confirmation took hours to arrive as the signal, in an effort to elude any human military screening, had to bounce around in a seemingly erratic pattern before reaching their homeworld, then back.

Einstein received the encrypted but unmistakable message straight to his BCI and his shoulders slumped. His suspicions were confirmed. He'd indeed found a female cyborg. Feet dragging, he moved to stand in front of his previously unknown lady. Raising fingers, which trembled slightly as emotions he couldn't name swamped him, he brushed at her cold cheek.

"Hello, B785, or should I call you Bonnie?" he said softly. "I'm sorry we didn't find you in time. I wish we could have helped you." Then in an impulse he didn't understand, he leaned forward and pressed his lips to hers in a gentle kiss.

A flare of something passed between them, a spark almost. However, that shock was nothing compared to the one he suffered when her eyes fluttered open.

Chapter Three

Darkness. She floated in darkness, a gentle ocean of nothingness and tranquility. Upon its gentle waves, she rested, relaxed in the cocooning embrace hugging her. Protecting her. Buffering her from the pain. The unfairness. She enjoyed the soothing touch. Never wanted to leave its comforting safety. But something disturbed her eternal rest. A voice, a gentle susurration, an insistent murmur penetrated the layers she'd sunk under, woke her, roused her consciousness…and stirred her curiosity.

She struggled to sink back down and remain in her deathlike trance, to recapture the peace of her final rest. However, the buzzing noise kept returning. Butterfly touches tickled her.

Like a flower unfurling in sunlight, or more aptly, the sleeping princess who wakens at the gentle kiss of her prince, her eyes popped open and she awoke.

The consternation on the face in front of her was almost comical, but not as hilarious as the male's embarrassment, which swiftly followed as he stumbled back. She cocked her head as the back of her unknown kisser's legs hit a precisely made bed and he fell upon it, arms and legs splaying in a most ungraceful manner. His mouth opened and shut, but no sound emerged, and yet, she could hear the sound of electronic devices and other noises perfectly fine. So the fault didn't lie with her auditory senses. It seemed shock caused him to lose his ability to speak. Perhaps if she put him at ease, he would utter something meaningful.

"Hello, handsome. In answer to your query, B785 is the name *they* gave me. I prefer to be called Bonnie," she answered in a soft voice that emerged more gravelly than she recalled, probably from disuse and a lack of moisture. Talk about waking up with a bad case of the pasties.

"You—But—How –?" Unable to string words in a coherent sentence, her rescuer, who'd managed to scramble into a seated position, blinked at her with bright blue, robotic eyes. They were kind of pretty, actually, bordered in thick, sinful lashes. She took in the rest of his facial features, from his straight nose to his angular cheeks and sensual lips, lips that moved with only the odd decipherable syllable emerging.

Entertaining or not, she decided not to wait and see if he ever located his power of speech. Running a quick overview of her status, she gauged her most urgent need. "Can I have some water?" she asked, as her internal diagnostics flagged the fluid as her most immediate need.

"Water?" he squeaked. "Of course. So sorry. Right away. Just give me a second." Off he dashed to a small sink in the corner. He returned quickly with a cup, the contents sloshing over the side. Her first attempt to grasp the drink failed, her stiff limbs not cooperating. The container splashed to the floor, wetting her bare feet. Her skin absorbed it like a sponge.

"Can I have more?"

Off he scurried again, refilling the cup, but this time, when he brought it back, he held it to her lips and she parted them, letting him pour the contents into her mouth. Swallowing, the fluid quickly got processed, along with the next few cups he poured into her mouth until she said, "Enough. I'm good."

"Do you need anything else? We don't have much in real food onboard, but I do have some minerals and other raw materials for you to digest."

How unappetizing, but necessary. She wrinkled her nose. "If you could. My resources are rather depleted."

The act of fetching her other items to ingest did much to help the male—*his name is Einstein,* her BCI supplied, vague memories of him speaking to her a dreamlike recollection—regain his composure. Or some of it at least. He still appeared quite agitated and ran his fingers through his light hair, ruffling it. She found his nervousness oddly quaint and a refreshing change from her final memories where the soldiers treated her as nothing better than an object for their use. Ugh. Now there was a memory she preferred to forget. Back into the room of things-she'd-rather-not-deal-with, she shoved it along with her sadness over Chloe's demise. She locked that door and concentrated on the present.

Humming underfoot seemed to indicate she was on some kind of vessel. A ship maybe? She was definitely in some kind of lab, the various computers and apparatus around her a familiar sight to someone used to almost daily testing. As she took in her surroundings, he gathered items and brought them to her, not meeting her gaze as he thrust them into her much steadier hands.

The powdery substances he handed her, ground nutrients that tasted of dry dust and chalk, didn't taste good, but her body took them all and used them to rebuild her strength, bringing her literally back to life. "Mmm. That's better," she eventually purred as her systems all came back online. "Thanks."

"You're welcome. I wish I'd known you were starving. I would have fed you. But I need to ask, how is this possible? I thought you were dead. All my testing and observations pointed to that conclusion."

"I was dead." *I think.* Bonnie still didn't understand what happened herself. One moment she existed in a dark limbo, a peaceful floating existence with no stress or pain or drama, the next…a voice spoke to her in the darkness. Asked questions she didn't answer. Touched her gently. Then, lips pressed against hers, lips sparking with something she'd not felt in ages. Something that woke her from her slumber despite her decision to end her life. "What did you do to wake me?"

Flustered, Einstein wouldn't meet her gaze. "About that… I, um, guess I should apologize for the liberty I took in kissing you. I would have never done that if I'd known you were still alive. It's just I found out who you were and –"

"Thought to play prince charming?" Her lips quirked at his gaping mouth as she once again rendered him speechless. "Don't tell me you're not familiar with the tale?"

He gathered himself. "No. I know the story, it's just I never expected you to wake up, not when everything else failed. It makes no logical sense."

"How would you know? Do you often go around kissing sleeping girls to see what happens?"

"No. Never. I've never kissed any female that I recall, as a matter of fact."

"Never?" Again, she teased him, which flustered him to no end. Oh the irony. She, a former high school slut, military whore, and all-around girl known for a good time, woken by an inexperienced geek. Bonnie let out a little laugh and stretched, limbs and muscles expanding like they hadn't in what seemed like ages, or more accurately, according to her onboard computer, three hundred and thirty-nine days, sixteen hours, and seven minutes.

"Are you teasing me?" he asked this with what seemed like sincere puzzlement, as if the very concept was foreign.

"Yes. Why? Is that a problem?"

"No. It's just, considering not even an hour ago you were dead to the world, I kind of would have expected—"

"More melodrama? Maybe some tears? I guess I could collapse into a weeping heap if you'd prefer, although it seems like a waste of water and time, if you ask me." She'd never found depression or hysterics accomplished anything. It was why she adopted a more of an *if you can't beat them, participate* motto early on when life took a drastic turn for the worse. She couldn't say it was much better, but at least then she felt in control, even if that control proved of her own imagining. She'd only given up when… Nope. Not going there. She wouldn't think of her reasons for putting herself in a deathlike coma.

"I guess."

Given his doubtful tone, she laughed. "Oh my, you're a cute one. Enough about me, though. Who are you?"

"I'm Einstein."

"As in the eccentric scientist?"

"More or less. It's the name I chose for myself when I liberated myself from the military programming imposed upon my mind. I used to be known as unit IQ221."

"Ooh, I hear a fascinating story behind that. You'll have to tell me about it later. First though, Einstein, formerly known as IQ221, where are we? And if you tell me in military custody, keep in mind I know a thousand ways to kill you." She winked, but her jest went right over his cute, tousled head.

He backed away, unable to hide his disconcert at her teasing claim. "We're on a military issue vessel, but it's not under human control anymore."

"You mean to say you and everyone aboard is cyborg? Fascinating." And unexpected. Last she'd heard, the orders came through to destroy them all. "But how? Did the military finally give the cyborgs their freedom? I never thought General Doom would. Last I remember, he seemed determined to either kill or hide his precious projects."

"You remember your time as a prisoner?"

Unfortunately. It was her turn to frown. "Of course I remember. It was one of the things that most vexed the bastard, the fact that no matter what he did, I refused to forget. Although, after awhile, I pretended to. One can only take so many sessions in the pit before you realize it's best to play along." Actually, it took losing her eyesight and getting outfitted with her robotic orbs for her to finally realize her stubborn stance needed revising.

The door to the room swished open without warning and they both swiveled to see who entered.

"Hey, Einstein old buddy, I just got the sad news—" The newcomer halted in the doorway and his eyes widened as he took her in.

Bonnie gave him the same once-over. Taller than her prince, the new cyborg possessed a thick head of hair cut in layers, a nice physique, and a bright white smile. In other words, he reminded her of a certain boring, yet popular doll whose type she remembered only too well. She understood this kind of male. If he were human, he'd be the kind of guy easy to manipulate, especially if promised sex. If he were human. Did male cyborgs share the same personality traits as their organic counterparts? Only one way to find out. "Hello, handsome. Nice of you to join the welcome party."

To his credit, the new guy didn't immediately fall for her charm. Nor did he address her directly. "She's alive?"

So much for smart. It seemed when the military created male cyborgs, they left out a few key ingredients such as intelligence. But hey, at least they left them with the ability to state the obvious. Bonnie linked her arm through Einstein's. "I am very much alive thanks to prince charming over here. He woke me with a heck of a kiss. Romantic, isn't it?"

"Einstein? Kissing? Dude, what the hell is she talking about?"

Poor Einstein, his poor BCI appeared to have gotten caught in a loop because he didn't answer. She took pity on her speechless rescuer. "*She* is called Bonnie and I already told you what happened. My sweet little geek over here gave me a smackeroo on the lips and woke me from my long sleep. I'll admit, I was surprised too, but, hey, shit happens. Now, since my prince seems at a loss for words, mind telling me who you are, where we are, and what the hell is going on?" She finished her demand on a questioning lilt.

"I'm Seth, head of covert operations, and this is Einstein, chief medical and communications officer. You are on the *SS BiteMe* under the command of Aramus, rudest bastard known in the cyborg world. But a decent shit nonetheless. Just don't ever tell him I said that."

"Seth!" Einstein rebuked him with just his name, not that the other male seemed to care, not if his wide grin was any indicator.

"What? I'm just telling her how it is. She's gonna meet our beloved commander any minute now. Best we brace her."

"Brace who for what?" bellowed a raspy voice. "I got a mental call to get my metal ass down here right away. This better be good, Seth, or I am going to pour water in your circuits just to watch you jiggle. Holy fucking shit." The big male who shoved his way into the room let out the curse along with a whistle.

Bonnie waved. "Hi there. You must be the boss of this operation. I'm Bonnie, formerly known as B785, or as the general liked to fondly call me, that irritating bloody bitch. But you can call me your newest pain in the ass." Then, she smiled broadly.

Chapter Four

Seeing Aramus speechless truly ranked high on the pleasure meter, as did his bulging eyes and the ticking nerve in his jaw. Of course, the captain of their mission, and king of acerbic comebacks, didn't let something like a presumed dead sexbot coming to life and taunting him keep him down for long.

"What the fuck is going on?"

"Einstein made out with what he thought was an inanimate droid and with the power of his super tongue—"

"Actually, he only used his lips," Bonnie interjected. "And he didn't even grope."

"—had a Prince Charming moment and woke the sleeping beauty who happens to be one of the missing cyborg women we've been looking for," Seth summarized with too much glee.

Aramus glared from Bonnie to Seth to Einstein, then back, and grunted. "Un-fucking believable. Why is it I keep ending up on the missions that find these cluster fucks? Why can't I ever enjoy a peaceful trip where the only excitement is blowing up some military scout ships and raiding some supply depots?"

Seth slapped Aramus on the back. "If you ask me, I think the scientists must have shoved some kind of lucky horseshoe up your tight ass. Adventuring with you is never boring."

"If you don't shut up, I'm going to shove something up yours," Aramus growled.

Seeing Bonnie's head bob back and forth as she took in the exchange between his two friends, Einstein wondered how it looked to her. Would she recognize the repartee of good friends or mistake it for the violence cyborgs were often accused of?

Using his wireless speech capability, Einstein sent a mental message. *"Hey, you two, would you stop that? She just woke up and I don't need you scaring her back to sleep."*

Seth immediately replied. *"But he started it."*

"And I'm asking you to stop it."

"Or else what?" Aramus mentally snarled.

"Hey, has anyone noticed that like Chloe and Fiona, she doesn't seem to have any wireless capability?"

Three pairs of eyes swung her way and Bonnie stiffened. "What? Why are you looking at me like that? Is there an asteroid chunk stuck in my teeth?"

"Did you hear any of that?"

"Any of what?"

"What our resident geek is trying to ask is if you have wireless capability?"

"Nope. None of the female cyborgs I knew did. The general said more than once that we were enough of a menace without giving us the ability to talk silently amongst ourselves."

"Finally, something a human said that I can agree with," Aramus replied.

Einstein elbowed him before Seth could, forcing an annoyed, "What? It's the truth."

"It is not," Einstein snapped, coming to the opposite sex's defense.

"Ha. You wait, boy. You'll soon come to see I'm right."

"Says a man who has never had a conversation with a woman that didn't send her screaming or crying in the other direction."

"And that's where you're wrong, because I don't bother talking to them in the first place," Aramus said with smug pride.

"One day…" Seth threatened.

"One day what?"

"One day, I hope a woman makes you eat your words."

"Never happen."

"Oh, it will. I've been wishing on every shooting star I see for it to happen."

"I'm going to beat you to a pulp."

"I'm going to beat you both to a pulp," Einstein said, annoyed at their constant bickering, and in front of their new guest, no less. "Sorry about that," he said to Bonnie. "I'd like to say they don't usually behave this way, but I hate to lie."

"Oh don't apologize for them. Anyone can see they argue because they secretly love each other."

Seth choked. Aramus' eyes bulged. Both exploded into a litany of denials while Bonnie watched with avid interest and a smirk on her lips. Einstein rubbed his face.

When did his carefully organized world devolve into chaos? Actually, Einstein knew that answer; the moment Bonnie regained her senses and stared at him with beautiful, emerald eyes.

Logical or not, the simple press of flesh against flesh should not have woken her. While he'd felt a strange electrical jolt on contact, he'd done nothing that would account for her suddenly coming to life. As for her comparison of their embrace to a fairy tale, magic didn't exist. Kisses didn't wake dead people, not even cyborg ones. *Tell that to Bonnie, though.* Because despite the implausibility, there she stood, antagonizing Aramus with sweet smiles and taunts. There she teased Seth with subtle innuendos that actually flustered the usually unflappable cyborg agent. There she was in bright living color, her skin tone already losing its gray pallor for a rosy hue, her cheeks plumping from all the minerals and fluid she'd imbibed, her flesh filling out rendering her less robot and more human. Womanly. Sexy. Troublesome. Intriguing…

"I think I need to sit down," Einstein announced to no one in particular. And he did, heavily. Knees weak, his mind caught in a loop as he struggled for logic, Einstein flopped down onto his mattress and tried to process the events. He failed, not something he was accustomed to, and he didn't appreciate it one bit. Unable to deal with the illogical series of events, he forced all the things

50

that refused to align into neat arrays to a corner of his mind for perusal when he had more time. Mind uncluttered, he focused on the more important matter at hand. Bonnie, and what to do with her.

Kiss her again in the name of science. And to see what would happen next. *Bzzzt!* Wrong answer. He shoved the inappropriate thought away, and sifted through the remaining ones, most improper—and surprising. They were relegated to a now crowded corner of his mind. Finally, one suggestion popped out that made the most sense—and caused him the least angst.

"Someone needs to let Chloe know her sister isn't dead after all."

The silence arrived so abruptly Einstein ran a quick internal check to see if his auditory functions still worked.

Bonnie cleared her throat. "Excuse me? Did you say Chloe? As in, my sister Chloe? As in my sister is still alive, Chloe?" Her voice got progressively louder, but that wasn't as daunting as the fact she took a step toward him with each query, her vivid eyes pinning him in place.

"If I say yes, are you going to hurt me?" Because she sure appeared ready to do violence, and Einstein doubted he could stop her. Not because he lacked the strength or ability, he just didn't think he could hurt her, not even in the name of self-defense.

Both her brows arched and she halted. "Hurt you? Only if you don't answer me. Tell me the truth. Is my sister alive?"

"Yes."

For a second, Einstein wondered if he'd sent her back into her catatonic state so still did she become. Bonnie took a deep, shuddering, and totally unnecessary breath. Nobody said a word as they waited for her to respond—or freak out.

Joy lit her face for a brief moment before her brows knit together in a fierce frown. "I'm going to kill that fucking bastard," she finally whispered. Lifting her head, her gaze fixed him, and despite the fact they were bionic, he could still see the pain reflected in her eyes and he disliked the fact he put it there. "He told me she was dead, you know. Gone. Never to be seen again. And he laughed about it. He fucking taunted me. The lying asshole. I should have known better than to believe anything that came out of his filthy fucking mouth. When I get my hands on him, I am going to feed him his balls. No, that's too nice. I'm going to rip out his entrails and hang him from them. Pour acid down his throat. Skin him alive…"

"Who?" Einstein dared to ask.

"The general, of course, the one in charge of the cyborg program, well, the female one at any rate. Sadistic bastard should have never messed with me." She paced as she threatened, an incongruous menace dressed only in a shirt with tousled hair and bare feet. If Einstein had a sense of humor, he might have found the image she presented amusing.

"Finally, she speaks a language I can understand," Aramus crowed.

"Does he have a name?" Seth interrupted.

"Or better yet, do you have a location?" Aramus asked as he slapped a fist into the palm of his hand. "I could use some stress relief."

"Well, I personally liked to call him asshole, but his actual name was General Vaughn. He was the bastard in charge of the female cyborg program."

"Never heard of him."

Einstein frowned. Nothing in his databanks flagged the name either. "What else can you tell us about him?"

"Tell? Well, he's old, probably in his sixties, but unlike his cronies, he didn't let himself go soft. The man's also colder than any machine he or his buddies ever created. I swear, the concept of emotion doesn't exist to him. And he called us the monsters."

"Was he a buddy of General Boulder?"

"Probably. Those military bastards are all in cahoots."

"Do you know where he is?"

"Not anymore, because I doubt he's still at the base he was using on earth. When I shut myself down, they were in the process of dismantling the location. Their funding got cut off. Apparently, they weren't working through legal government channels and got caught funneling funds. They had to close up shop and quick. I never did get wind of where they were going next, just the rumors that basically said they were destroying the evidence of our existence and relocating the scientists who worked on the project."

"Joe is going to want to know about this," Seth replied.

"Joe? Who's Joe?" she asked, halting her pacing tracks.

Einstein answered now that he no longer feared her wrath. "Joe's the leader of the cyborg liberation movement. He's also the chosen partner of your sister. They live together on the world we've commandeered."

"My sister is married?" The note of incredulity made her seem all too human.

"Of a sorts. Joe and your sister share a deep affection for each other and cohabit."

"They're in love," Seth sang, accompanied by kissing noises.

"I'll be damned," Bonnie said in a low tone, not seeming upset at the news, more in awe. "It's about time she found herself a man. She always was the shy one. You'll have to tell me about this Joe guy who managed to steal her heart. Actually, I want to know everything you can tell me about her and what's happened while I was sleeping. Better yet, when do I get to see her and meet her fellow?" A hopeful smile curled her lips, and captivated Einstein.

"Three weeks, seven days, fourteen hours, give or take," Aramus answered.

"That long!" Crestfallen, Bonnie's shoulders slumped. Einstein almost reached out to her in comfort, an illogical gesture, especially coming from him. He pulled his hand back before it made contact. She must have caught on to his aborted action, though, and in a surprise move, flopped onto his lap and lay her head on his shoulder. Einstein went still. "Can't you make it faster, charming?"

"No, he can't," growled Aramus. "Protocol must be followed. We have to ensure the military hasn't tracked us from our last location and we still need to pick up some supplies before heading back."

"Track you from where? Did you attack a military base? Raid a supply depot? Hit them somewhere it will hurt?"

"Not exactly." Einstein didn't elaborate.

Seth did. "We've just come from a floating pleasure palace where the troops enjoyed some stress relief. It's where we found you, princess."

Bonnie stiffened and tilted her face at Einstein, accusation in her glare. "You found me in a brothel?"

He nodded.

"Pig. And I thought you were different." She shoved off his lap, leaving Einstein at a loss for her sudden annoyance. He'd done nothing wrong. Actually, if he examined the situation, she should thank him for having attended the brothel because if he hadn't, she would have soon ended up as space debris. Of course, he didn't say any of this aloud. He didn't need to justify his actions. She was the one acting irrational.

As if to make up for his error, Seth spoke up in his defense. "Hey, before you get your circuits in a knot, you should know that Einstein here is the only one who wasn't partaking of the flesh available. Which is completely unnatural, if you ask me. He spent his entire time in the repair center fixing broken sexbots."

"Truly?" She turned to him for verification.

All Einstein managed was a nod.

His simple reply made her beam, a bright expression short-lived. A frown soon marked her countenance. "But I don't understand. How did I end up in a bordello? Please don't tell me I was being used as some kind of inanimate sex doll. I mean, I'm all for fucking. Heck, I've had more than my share of group sex marathons, but I prefer to participate. Or at least keep count of who's heaving over me."

The odd warmth in his cheeks returned. Einstein peered at his feet before answering. "As far as I know, you weren't used in that manner. I found you crated in a box. The owner had you slated to go in the trash because he couldn't get you activated. He gave you to me in payment for my service."

She planted her hands on her hips and eyed him sternly. "And what exactly did you plan to use me for?"

"Not for sex," he hastened to say.

She laughed. "Why not? Aren't I pretty enough? And before you answer, don't forget, I already know you kissed me, charming."

"Oh make me puke bolts," Aramus grumbled. "I am not listening to this. I'm out of here. I'm sure there's something more important needing my attention. Like counting the rivets in the repair bay."

"I'll tell you what's more important, getting some decent porn to watch. Did you know all we've got onboard are educational videos?" Seth harangued Aramus as he followed him out the door, and Einstein sighed as he heard Aramus growl, "I'm going to rip your leg off and beat you with it."

"Only if you catch me first, which as you well know, is unlikely given you're a first generation model. Why that makes you practically my grandfather."

The door slid shut, cutting off further sound, leaving them alone –something Einstein became only too aware of, especially given he still sat while she stood. Stood in only a thin shirt. A barely there fabric barrier that did nothing to truly conceal the curve of her breasts or the flash of her thighs. He averted his gaze, not sure why her partial dishabille made him so uncomfortably aware. He'd had no problem ignoring her attributes before. *Of course, before, she was just an inanimate object.* Now…now she was one hundred percent woman, and it seemed he was more human and male than he'd suspected.

"I'm waiting?" she said in the sudden silence.

"Waiting for what?"

"An answer of course, my prince. You never did reply. Why did you want me? Why save me from ignoble death by trash compacter if you didn't have plans to debauch my lifeless, yet delectable body?" She returned to his lap, this time straddling and facing him.

It threw him for a loop, especially when he felt an inappropriate twitch from his lower parts. An erection? *Stand down.* His mental command did nothing to reduce the swelling. He could only hope she didn't notice.

She cupped his cheeks and forced him to face her. "Eyes on me, charming. No going off into a loop. I'm still waiting for an answer on why you brought me to your lab."

A partial truth tumbled out. "I thought I could use your for parts." As if he'd admit curiosity played the biggest role.

"Parts?" The fingers toying with the ends of his hair stilled. "Did you say parts as in dismantle me and divvy me up among other cyborgs? Are you sure your name isn't Frankenstein?"

"If you are referring to the doctor in the fiction story, then his name was actually…" He stopped talking at her arched brow. "Oh, I guess that's not pertinent to your query. I acquired you in the hopes of seeing if I could reanimate you, or that was the plan at first, and only if I couldn't would I have looked at using you for parts."

"Eew." Her nose wrinkled, which should have rendered her less attractive. It didn't. He swelled a little more to his embarrassment. He really, really hoped she didn't feel a thing, but somehow, the squirm on his lap and smirk on her lips seemed to indicate otherwise.

"I wasn't done explaining. As you can tell, that obviously didn't happen. The more I studied you, the more it occurred to me that you weren't a droid like I first thought. You had too many anomalies. So I tried to run some diagnostics to test a theory that perhaps you were a cyborg, however, I ran into issues. In order to keep the damage to your physical exterior to a minimum, I needed better equipment, but that would have meant waiting weeks until we got back to my permanent lab."

"So how did you figure out who I was?"

"It was actually Seth who came up with the simplest solution. We sent your picture back to our homeworld and ran it by Fiona and Chloe to see if they recognized you. Once your sister confirmed your identity…" He shrugged. "Well, you know the rest."

She sighed. "You really know how to sweet talk a girl, don't you, charming?"

"I'm afraid I don't follow."

"So I'm beginning to notice." She flowed off his lap to pace his lab. For one illogical moment, he almost tugged her back, missing the weight and closeness. "Where do we go from here?"

"First, we're heading to an asteroid belt in the Beta quadrant."

"Hold on one second. Did you say asteroid, as in space asteroid?"

"Of course. As Seth told you, you're aboard the *SS Bite Me*, which you should know was not my first choice in name, but I got outvoted."

"We're on a spaceship?" She practically yelled the question.

"Yes." Why she kept asking, he couldn't figure out unless she'd sustained some damage to her short term memory banks.

"Holy shit. I thought you meant we were on a ship, ship. You know, the kind that floats on the ocean."

"What an odd assumption."

She planted her hands on her hips. "I resent that. I mean, how was I supposed to know we were in space? Last thing I remember, I was a gazillion levels below ground in some secure military base."

"They moved you."

"Obviously," she drawled. "Space, huh? The final frontier… Fucking awesome. Can I see?"

"See what?" She changed subject so quickly, Einstein struggled to follow.

"The stars, of course. The galaxy. Space stuff. I always wanted to be one of the lucky ones who got to leave Earth, but given my *behavioral issues*—" She waggled her fingers to simulate air quotes. "General Doom always refused."

"I don't have a viewing screen in this room, as you can see; however, other areas of the ship do have portholes and viewing areas. I will show them to you if you'd like."

"Would I ever! Ha. Me in space. Too fucking wild. Hey, does that make me an astronaut?"

"I guess." He thought it best to humor her, especially since the idea seemed to bring her so much pleasure, or so he assumed as she began humming the theme song from an old earth television series titled *Star Trek*.

"I'm gonna see the stars. Maybe find some aliens. Seek out new worlds." She sang the words and danced around, strangely elated. He didn't interrupt. Given her mood swings, he thought it safer. When she stopped spinning, she faced him again. "Well, at least now your whole timeline makes more sense. I guess we can't just hop a plane and get to my sister. I mean, I assume she's not on earth then?"

"Not even close."

"She lives on an alien planet? Oh this is getting cooler and cooler."

"I wouldn't call it alien. The biology of it is similar in many respects to earth with adequate gas levels, plantation, and simple animal life."

"But it's not earth."

"No, it's not."

"Can I see that too?"

"We don't have images stored on this vessel in case we're boarded by hostiles, but I can describe it to you." A pity she didn't have a wireless link, he could have sent her some of the images of their homeworld stored in his memory banks.

"I'd like that. And I'll get to live there too?"

"Once we can ascertain our path is clear."

"Awesome." Her smile stretched and he couldn't help but reply in kind, her enthusiasm over her new status contagious. "Okay, so back to my previous question before I got distracted. Now that I'm awake, what's next?"

"According to our schedule, the ship will enter the Beta quadrant, which is rich in meteors. Several in particular have been marked for exploitation. After we mine some needed ores from the surface, we'll be heading—"

"I didn't mean for you to give me an actual itinerary." She laughed. "Someone really needs to teach you not to take everything so literally."

A grimace tugged at his lips as she pointed out his flaw. "I know. Seth's been trying to educate me, but unlike some of the others who've found their humanity, mine was completely wiped." A fact he didn't usually lament, except for now. He sensed some odd undercurrent between him and the female cyborg. A tug on his senses, a quickening of his pulse, a stir of his usually well behaved cock. He wished he knew what it meant. Unlike Joe, Solus, and a few of his other brothers, Einstein didn't fool himself into believing he could ever feel affection, or love. The military changed him too much and his analytical mind understood all too well that emotion was just a result of hormones and pheromones becoming unbalanced. Despite his current malfunction, he'd soon adjust and go back to his usual, rational self, an observer and a scientist in perfect control of all his bodily functions and emotions.

Apparently, Bonnie harbored different plans. "We'll just see about that. I think you might be more human inside than you realize. You just need the right person and incentive to bring it out."

If Einstein didn't know better, he'd suspect she thought she held the skills to do just that. And yet, he didn't get the impression she was a doctor or technician. Exactly how she planned to program him was a mystery, one he didn't dare question, not given the way her mood swung.

As if to prove his point about her irrational nature, she changed the subject. "Where's the nearest shower? I smell like dust and I swear I'm wearing an inch of filth."

"In the corner of the room. But, if you give me a moment, I'll reassign a few of my brethren and give you a room of your own."

"Reassign as in move some of the onboard cyborgs elsewhere?"

"Yes."

"Where will they go?"

"To another room. I'll double up a pair in other quarters."

"Oh no. Don't do that. There's nothing worse than forcing some guys to give up their space for a girl. That's all I need is to have the crew resent me because you're cramming them like sardines into a room."

"We wouldn't cram them. The space is ample for cohabiting if we put the units on opposing, rotating shifts."

"You really don't have a clue, do you?" She shook her head, smiling at his words as if she found them humorous, yet an analysis showed no jest that he could find. "Do you have a roommate?"

"Not currently."

"Then how come I can't just stay here?"

"Here?" In his lab? "I guess I could sleep elsewhere, however, I'd have to return for work as most of the equipment is restricted to this location."

"You're being literal again. I mean, why can't I stay here with you? I won't get in your way or take up much room. And I trust you. Any guy who can go to a bordello and stick to fixing naked pussy instead of fucking it can surely be trusted not to molest me while I sleep or shower."

"I would never touch you inappropriately." Seth would have been proud of his indignant retort.

"Says the guy who kissed me."

"An anomaly, I swear. It won't happen again."

"A shame. But not to worry, I don't intend to make any such promises." She winked, but before Einstein could reply or ask her to elaborate on what she meant, off came the shirt she wore in a flutter of fabric. He watched with more interest than it warranted the gentle sway of her hips as she headed for the shower cubicle in the corner. Why did the appearance of her naked buttocks make his cock swell? He'd never noticed a female's posterior before. But that was before. Awake only a short while and yet, since the female cyborg's emergence from her comalike state, everything had changed for him, which made absolutely no sense.

He'd seen B785—*she prefers Bonnie*—naked before. Gone over every inch of her, actually, both visually and physically, during his attempts to reanimate, but now…now everything had altered. He couldn't have said why. Was it because her skin glowed with health? Because her limbs flowed with sensual grace? Because she threw him a coy smile over her shoulder and licked her lips? Was it a combination of all these factors that brought a flush to his cheeks? The answer eluded him, but he could state for a fact that it was the twitch of his cock, an erection he neither commanded nor controlled, that sent him fleeing his room, the sound of her laughter trailing behind him.

Unfortunately, while he could escape her physical presence, he could do nothing to erase her from his mind. On the contrary, she overtook his thoughts, a fast-acting virus that consumed him with lusty ideas and images. A plague on his usually well ordered slate of a mind, but one he didn't want to wipe clean.

Chapter Five

Alone in the shower, a small cubicle with just enough room to wash, Bonnie pondered the strangeness of the circumstances she'd woken to. Despite her light jests, surprise didn't come close to describing her emotions when she awoke to a gentle kiss. And the surprises kept mounting.

The cyborgs had freed themselves from military control. They governed themselves. They'd formed a society. They'd found her sister and one other, Fiona, a tough female whom as she recalled, always stood up for them. Bonnie had thought the woman destroyed. It made her glad to know she survived. But her happiness at the news didn't compare to the elation at discovering Chloe lived.

My sister is alive! Alive and in love by the sounds of it. If she could have cried in relief and joy, she would have. Damned robotic eyes. Yet despite the lack of tears, she sobbed inside. For so long, she'd carried the burden of guilt of having brought her sister to the general's attention. It was after all Bonnie's fault they'd ended up in that hospital.

"Thanks for coming to get me," Bonnie had slurred from the passenger seat of her sister's car.

"You didn't leave me much choice," Chloe replied tersely, keeping her eyes on the road.

"Not my fault I lost my cab money. I had it stashed in my bra. Must have fallen out." Or gotten stolen by one of the guys groping her in a dark corner. Who knew? Who cared?

Apparently, Chloe did. "Bonnie, you can't keep doing this. You're a grown woman."

"And? There's nothing wrong with having a little fun."

"There is when you're about to lose your job again because you got drunk and won't make it in to work for the third time this month."

"You're such a sp-spoilsport." Damned tricky words struggled to make it past her thick tongue.

"It's called being responsible."

Bonnie blew a raspberry at her sister. "Bah. We're young. There's plenty of time to get boring later. I want to have fun." She kicked her legs and stubbed her toe on the dash. Ow.

A sigh left Chloe. "And how many guys did you have fun with this time?"

Bonnie didn't want to admit she didn't know. It would lend a little too much ammo for her buzz kill of a sister's argument. "Hey, the more the merrier. You should try it sometime. A good, old fashioned gang bang might loosen you up." Bonnie leered at her.

Chloe's lips tightened. "No, thank you. Some of us prefer to be choosier about our partners."

"Prude."

"Slut." The vulgar word, so crude and unexpected, hung in the air between them. Hurtful. True. A slap that

67

almost sobered her. Anger swept through Bonnie, anger and…shame.

"God, I hate you when you get all fucking self-righteous. Who are you to judge me? I'm not hurting anyone."

"You're hurting yourself."

"So what? It's my choice."

"One you keep dragging me into," Chloe pointed out through gritted teeth. "Usually at three am when I should be sleeping. Unlike you, I intend to make it to work and my classes on time. But now, I get to write an exam on little to no sleep because, once again, you couldn't control yourself."

"I don't have to listen to this. Let me out." Bonnie struggled with the door latch, only to realize her sister had locked it.

"Stop that. You're not getting out. I'm taking you home."

"Well I don't want to go home now. Not with you." A part of Bonnie recognized she was acting childish, but the alcohol encouraged her petulance. "Let me out."

"No."

"Yes." Bonnie lunged for the steering wheel. She knew it was wrong and dangerous, but she couldn't help herself. Poor Chloe, she tried to fend her off, tried to keep them on the road, tried to avoid the telephone pole…

Bonnie's shoulders shook as she sobbed in the shower, reliving, as she had hundreds of times, the actions that had cost her sister a normal life. If only she'd said no to the invitation to go to the bar. If only she'd borrowed money and called a cab instead of Chloe for a ride. If only…she'd led a different life.

Waking in the hospital, weeks—or was it months later?—different, enhanced, no longer completely human, she'd raged against what the military did to them. So what if they claimed to have saved their lives, they'd also ruined them. By changing them into partial machines, they'd made it impossible for Chloe to have the happiness she deserved. But worst of all was what they subjected them to after.

Bonnie could handle the leering men and the sexual expectations. Sure, she didn't have the buffer of alcohol and drugs to soften the comments and acts, but she'd been around enough to handle the emotional and physical rape. But poor Chloe. She never deserved it.

But she's found happiness finally, despite it all. Or so Einstein claimed. Oddly, despite her ill experiences at the hands of men, she believed him. He possessed too much honesty to lie. Too much naivety to make it up. However, despite what he claimed, Bonnie wouldn't truly believe it until she saw Chloe for herself and heard from her lips that she was happy. *And if she isn't?*

I'll do something about it. Because she owed it to her.

Toweling off, she rummaged through Einstein's drawers, smirking at his neatly folded shirts and pants. Given his height, she didn't bother with the cargo pants, no way would they fit. She opted for a sleeveless tee, a button-up linen shirt, and underneath those, a pair of boxers, which she tightened around her waist using a belt she found and modified to fit her more slender frame. For her feet, she slid on a pair of socks, not because the cold floor bothered her, but because she felt less vulnerable that way. From the sounds of it, she was the only woman on a ship full of men.

A smart girl would have probably stayed hidden in her room. However, Bonnie never did like to do the smart thing. She sauntered forth to explore and as usual, it didn't take long for trouble to find her.

*

Einstein initially thought to make his way to the bridge, but riled up and in possession of a strange, tense energy, he diverted his path instead to the onboard gym where he found Seth sparring with another cyborg named Aphelion. Less sparring and more like wiping the mat with him. No one quite knew what type of programming Seth possessed. Of all the cybernetic units, he proved impenetrable to testing, but despite the fact they couldn't download his programming or delve through the cybernetic options he'd been embedded with, Seth proved time and time again that he was cyborg to the core despite his more than human exterior.

"Einstein? What are you doing here? I would have thought you'd be occupied with our lady guest. And by occupied, I mean *occupied*."

Seth's brows waggled and Einstein couldn't stop the heat from rising in his cheeks. He really needed to run a diagnostic on his systems, or program a sub routine to root out the imperfection in his BCI causing him to succumb to embarrassment.

"Bonnie wanted a shower."

"You've got a naked, wet female in your room and you left?"

"Yes."

"Dude, what is wrong with you?"

"It's called being courteous. You should try it sometime."

"Ouch!"

Einstein couldn't tell if he meant the blow Aphelion landed or his remark.

"Since she wouldn't let me assign her a room of her own and insisted on staying with me, I thought it polite to leave and give her some privacy to bathe."

"You dog!" Seth flattened his opponent and straightened with a wide grin. "She's staying with you? Good for you, dude."

"Why is that good?"

"Because. Isn't this part of your master plan to seduce her and live happily ever after? She did call you her prince charming."

"Her continual reference to the fairy tale is obviously a sign of trauma to her central core. I've already filed a mental report to run a full evaluation on her programming to root out the obvious defects. As for assigning her other quarters, as I mentioned, I tried. She wouldn't let me."

71

"Why not?" Seth asked as he pummeled the punching bag in a blurring rhythm no one could match.

"She says reassigning troops would cause resentment and that she trusts me to share my quarters with her."

Halting his rhythmic punches, Seth turned to face him. "Ugh, dude. That sucks."

"Why? I do not mind sharing the space. It is more than ample for the both of us."

"Not that. The old I trust you bit. You know what that means."

"You are alluding to something that I think goes beyond her actual words."

"I am. It means she thinks you're not going to put the moves on her. That she sees you as a *friend.*" Seth's nose wrinkled.

"How is that bad?"

"Because how are you going to get in her pants if she doesn't think of you as something more?"

Einstein wisely didn't point out the obvious. One, she didn't have any pants, and two, why would he want to get in them? Wouldn't the sharing of slacks be uncomfortable? Sometimes, it was just easier to act as if he understood. "If having her as a roommate proves too disruptive, then I'll just reassign her to other quarters. I'm sure I can devise an excuse if required."

"Or she'll shack up with another cyborg on her own."

Familiar with that particular bit of slang, Einstein, in the midst of doing pushups, lost his rhythm and hit the mat—with his face. He waited for the laughter and when none came, lifted his visage to see Seth facing away working on another exercise device.

Spared the embarrassment, he rolled to his back and proceeded to stretch and work his abdominal muscles. "If Bonnie chooses to form an attachment to an onboard unit, then I will respect her choice."

"Will you?"

"Of course. Why would I not?"

"Because you found her. Because you kissed her awake."

Because she's mine. Where did the random thought come from? As if Einstein, or any cyborg for that matter, owned anybody. As free-thinking entities, they belonged to themselves. "I have no need for a female in my life."

"Says the virgin," scoffed Seth.

"I am not a virgin. I've experienced coitus. I just don't see the big deal."

"Then you didn't do it right."

"I ejaculated."

"But you didn't come."

"What's the difference?"

"If you'd truly had sex, I wouldn't have to explain it. Lucky you, though, you've got the prime opportunity to finally get rid of your pesky inexperience. Bonnie is prime girlfriend material. And if you don't do something to make your interest in her clear, she's going to find someone else."

Taking a page from Seth's book on humanisms, Einstein replied, which was to say, he didn't answer at all. "Whatever."

A blasé response, but it shut Seth up. They continued their work out, switching their conversation to other topics. However, Seth's words kept repeating themselves over and over. For some reason, they bothered Einstein. He couldn't have said why. His existence didn't require the addition of sex or a female to complete or enrich it. He was perfectly content with his current status. If that was the case, though, why did he imagine he could hear a loud buzzer of denial every time he told himself that?

An answer to that question remained out of reach, no matter how hard he worked his body and attempted to remove the excess adrenaline from his system. Opting to use the shower in the gym to sluice off, and the spare clothes found there, he delayed the return to his quarters as long as possible, ostensibly to give her some privacy even if the definition of cowardice kept taunting him.

Dressed, exercised, and unable to remain in the gym any longer without question, Einstein left only to veer down the corridor away from his room. *I should check on the bridge.* Never mind he held a direct wireless link to the shipboard computer, a visit in person seemed called for.

He heard Aramus bellowing before he reached the bridge.

74

"This area is off limits."

Why did it not surprise him to hear the dulcet voice of his dilemma reply, "Why? Is it for boys only? Are you all hanging around in your underwear telling fart jokes? I can fart on demand if I have to. Heck, I can even belch the alphabet. Want to hear?"

"No!"

A tiny chuckle escaped him at Aramus' disgusted retort. Swinging around the corner, he came across the arguing pair. Bonnie saw him before his captain did and smiled. "Charming, there you are. I've been looking all over for you. Grumpy pants here wouldn't tell me where you went."

"Onboard personnel locations are private. In other words, if Einstein wanted you to fucking know where he was, he would have told you."

Bonnie stuck her tongue out at Aramus and Einstein stepped between them when it looked as if Aramus might forget she was a lady—albeit a mouthy one determined to get throttled.

"I was in the gym. Sorry. I forgot we're not linked on a neural level and I didn't yet have a chance to program you for onboard communication access." Just another deficiency to add to his growing list.

"You are not giving her access." Aramus crossed his arms over his chest and glowered at the petite female.

"Why not?" Einstein asked.

"Because for all we know, she's a military spy."

"A spy?" She laughed. "What part of I hate those bastards and they were glad to be rid of me did you not grasp?"

"Says you."

"Says anyone. If you could access my files, you'd know the general abhorred me. He'd never use me as a spy because I am more likely to feed him false information so I can watch him fail than to give him anything he could use to hurt anyone."

"Again, says you. Besides, even if you are telling the truth, it doesn't mean you're not a secret spy. How do we know you're not a carrier of some bug, or tracking device?"

"Now you're grasping," she said with a roll of her eyes, a disconcertingly human motion given their robotic gleam. "You found me in a box gathering dust in a brothel. I'd say the chances of your theory panning out are slim to none."

"But possible."

Einstein watched them argue back and forth, staying out of the heated debate until they both turned to him and said, almost in unison, "Can you show him/her wrong?"

Stubborn, meet equally stubborn. And lucky him, they'd chosen Einstein to mediate. "I've yet to detect anything out of the ordinary."

"However, it's possible, right?" Aramus pressed.

"I guess."

"Oh, you would take his side," she huffed, crossing her arms. "Men always stick together."

"I said possible, but in my opinion, unlikely," he added, wiping the smirk off Aramus' face only to plant a smug expression on Bonnie's.

"So how do we settle this? I don't want this *female,*" Aramus sneered, "having access to our secrets until we know for sure."

"I'm already monitoring for signals. I ran all the scans I could when she was inert."

"But none since she woke up."

"No."

"So test me then," she offered, opening her arms wide. "Strip me naked and probe me, charming. I've got nothing to hide."

"Here? Now?" His high-pitched squeak didn't resemble his usual voice at all.

"Of course not here, silly. Back in your lab. As if I'd give Mr. I-Think-I'm-So-Mighty a peek at this body after the way he's treated me."

"Treated you? You're lucky I didn't lock you up. If I had my way, you'd be in chains undergoing a debriefing, but apparently, that would be cruel."

"Aramus!"

"What? I said I wanted to, not that I was going to."

Why did Einstein have an urge to bang his head on a wall? Violence to his cranium wouldn't solve anything.

"Kinky, are you, captain? I'll bet the ladies love that."

"As if you'd know anything about ladies," Aramus retorted.

"Touché. But back to the spy thing. You have questions. Ask away. I have nothing to hide."

"I doubt that." Aramus, true to form, didn't trust anyone. Einstein often wondered why. Just what had the big cyborg suffered in his past to make him so leery of anyone, even his own kind? And especially women.

"Wow, I don't know where you were when they handed out the nice guy microchip, but apparently, you should have stood in line for two. You are some kind of suspicious."

"Just following protocol, Pita."

"Pita?" Her nose wrinkled. "My name is Bonnie."

"Not to me you aren't. In my books, you're P. I. T. A. PITA as in pain in the ass."

With that, Aramus whirled on his heel and stalked off, leaving Einstein alone with Bonnie, who giggled. "Wow, is he ever easy to rile up."

"He has his reasons. Not everyone made the transition from mindless droid to sentience with ease. Some woke with memories best left buried. Aramus was one of them." Even if the surly droid denied it. Aramus claimed to not remember anything, but his attitude spoke of a grudge. However, Einstein respected his right to privacy. They all did.

"I suffered too. It doesn't mean I turned into a righteous bitch."

"Then you're luckier than many. Some found the memories of their past and indoctrination with the military too much. Many went insane when they remembered what was done to them." The suicide rate in that first year and kamikaze missions was statistically high for a population their size, but in the years since had thankfully settled down. They still had the occasional cyborg snapping, or sporting a quick temper, but most came to some kind of grip with their past lives and moved on.

"Poor bots," she murmured. "I guess I can understand that. Fiona and some of the others went through some rough shit, rough enough that forgetting was probably a blessing in disguise. Even Chloe began to blank out in the end."

"And you?"

Bonnie sighed, a sad sound so unlike her usual bubbly nature. "Cursed with the memory of an elephant. Defective, as the doctor used to say every time he tried to program me into being the perfect little soldier."

"How did they program you? I saw no sign of an exterior port and you exhibit no wireless signal."

"I already told you. None of the females had wireless. General Doom claimed he wasn't making that mistake again. When the docs needed to upgrade my software, they used to slice me open right behind the ear. I've got a micro connector embedded back there for hard wiring."

"When we get back to our planet, if you don't mind, I'd like to connect our computer to you. We've been trying to gather as much info as possible about the different cyborg units. While we have the males pretty much figured out, the female units seem to all have different characteristics."

"Every flavor possible," she joked. "We were the general's experiment. No two female cyborgs were made alike."

"Why?"

She shrugged. "Your guess is as good as mine."

As they walked back to his lab, he questioned her, in the name of science, of course. "How did you come to the military's attention?"

"I got drunk one night and caused an accident while my sister was driving. They said it was bad. I don't know. I don't remember any of that. They kept me pretty drugged up. When I woke up, I was part machine, a whole lot of pissed, and a prisoner of the military. You?"

"I have no memories of my time before, but from what I've gleaned on the files I accessed, I was a juvenile delinquent in foster care who came to their attention because I hacked a secure website."

"Must have been some hack."

"Apparently, the CIA took offense at a fourteen-year-old getting past their safeguards."

She whistled. "Holy shit. They got to you young. How old are you now?"

"According to records? Twenty-five. Apparently, they kept me incarcerated for quite a number of years before entering me in the cyborg program."

"No wonder you're so clueless. You never really had a chance to live." Her sad tone made him shift uncomfortably. Used to his past, he'd never before had someone pity him for it. Most envied him his intelligence.

Uncomfortable with the turn in conversation, he took an example from her and changed the subject. "You said the military gave the females different aspects. What abilities did you get?"

"I got a smorgasbord. Quick healing. Impervious to pain. An enhanced skeletal structure and embedded armor around my ribcage."

"They put a shield around the organs in your torso?" Einstein couldn't hide his scientific curiosity at such a strange concept.

"Yup. They wrapped me in some kind of weird metal, shaped to look like a rib cage and stuff, then covered it back over in skin, tissue, and muscle. Pretty neat, huh? And you'd think it would be hell on metal detectors, but somehow, I don't know how they did it; you can't tell it's there at all on x-rays."

Hell indeed since it meant she could hide anything within the metallic cocoon. Something of his dismay must have shown on his face.

Her smile faded. "Shit. I just proved Captain Rude right, didn't I? I could have some bug inside me or something worse hiding, waiting to blow us all up."

"Surely you would have noticed given you seem to have retained all your memories."

"The memories of my time before I shut myself down. Who knows what the general did to my body after I turned my will to live off?"

Einstein tried to reassure her. "Placing an explosive or any tracking device within you seems like a waste of technology if you were slated for destruction. Not to mention, if he had a way to locate you, why would he wait until now to use it? If we assume you were hijacked by pirates and sold to the brothel as stolen merchandise, then surely the general would have activated it by now and retrieved you." Or blown her up so make sure the wrongs hands didn't get a hold of her.

"You know what they say about assumptions." At his blank look, she shook her head. "I'll explain later. In the meantime, we have to go with what we know. And that's very little since my blackout. While I slept, how do we know what happened to me? Aramus is right to be suspicious. Heck, I don't completely trust you guys yet. For all I know, you're lulling me into a false sense of security so you can hand deliver me to the devil."

"Never." A vehement reply, which tumbled without thought from his lips.

"I know you think that, but who knows what programming time bombs remain planted, hidden in our BCIs waiting for the right moment to explode."

"I assure you, my mind harbors no hidden subroutines. I'd have found them by now."

"Has anyone ever told you how cute you are when you talk like a geek?" She grinned at him and Einstein ducked his head, pleased at her mention of cute. "Enough chit-chat, charming. Time for action. You promised the boss you'd probe me."

"We don't have to."

"Oh, but I insist."

"I'll be as unobtrusive as possible," he promised.

"Well, that's no fun," she pouted, skipping alongside him.

No fun was going to be him trying to not view her as a woman. Alive, full of energy, and intriguing in so many ways, Einstein wondered how he'd get through an intense examination because just the mere thought had his malfunctioning dick semi-erect.

Maybe he should be the one submitting himself for an exam with her at the helm. *Because I'll bet she makes a sexy nurse.*

Chapter Six

Entering the workshop, which doubled as his medical lab, Bonnie wasted no time hopping up onto the metal table set to the side of the room. It amused her to see how nervous Einstein appeared, how he wouldn't meet her eyes as he gathered some tools and equipment, how he tried to hide the fact he sported a woody.

Cute didn't come close to describing him. She already loved how his neatly cut, light brown hair got the ruffled appearance she was starting to realize signaled his agitation. *I make him anxious.* His reaction to her was so unlike the men she used to know. Most of the doctors in her past didn't bother to hide their leering looks or temper their sexual comments. They made medical exams and tests into something dirty, touching her more than necessary, stroking and pinching for a reaction. Einstein, on the other hand, tried to get away with not palpating her at all.

Talk about totally ruining her fun. Heck, he even gave her a sheet to wear when she stripped down, his red cheeks—so unexpected in a cyborg—the only indication that he'd caught a peek at her assets. Why she wanted him to notice her as more than a test subject she couldn't have explained. Perhaps it was the challenge he posed. Or the fact she could tell he wanted her but fought it. *Or maybe it's just plain hormones.* After all, when was the last time she'd had sex, or even wanted sex for that matter? Funny how the one guy who got her motor running—and not just the mechanical one— was the one guy immune to the sexual vibes she kept tossing his way. *I guess I'll have to try harder.* But seriously, how could he not be aware of her interest? Pulse elevated, temperature running high, and her nipples pebbled, the physical indications were all there for him to see. And apparently ignore.

At the same time she lamented the lack of sexual action, she also couldn't forget the reason for the exam. Had the general planted a nasty surprise in her body? Was she a walking time bomb? An inadvertent spy? She needed to find out and before they met up with her sister. Knowing she was alive and in love brought such a sense of relief. Despite her fuckup, Chloe was getting her happily ever after and Bonnie wouldn't ruin it. So despite her urge to make the testing into something more carnal, she held back and let Einstein do his job. Plenty of time to seduce her geeky scientist once they knew she wouldn't explode or lead the military to her sister.

Prone on his table, legs slightly spread, she let him run various scans, bored and silent, aware that the vibrations of her voice would disrupt some of the more delicate equipment. But when he finally got around to the hands-on part, with an apologetic, "Sorry if my fingers are cold," she couldn't help teasing him.

"I know a way to warm them up."

"I'll run them under warm water."

"That's not what I was thinking. I've got more than enough heat right here and I don't mind sharing," she replied with a wink.

"Is your temperature control malfunctioning?" he asked with a serious mien. "I don't have one myself, the military not deeming it necessary for someone of my skills, but I've worked on some with the other units."

Bonnie almost slapped herself as he misread her once again. Surely he wasn't that clueless? Looking at his waiting expression, she realized, yeah, he was. But how? Sure, the military snagged him young, but still, Einstein was a man, and not an unattractive one. Surely he'd dated, or at the very least had a nurse or two come on to him. "How come I get the impression you're not too experienced when it comes to girls?"

The fingers skimming her ribcage faltered. "My work keeps me busy and I've never seen a need to exert myself with the opposite sex. I have few biological needs."

"You're a virgin?" No fucking way.

The comment made him fidget. "Not exactly. I do have some experience."

"Obviously not very good ones, given your lack of enthusiasm for a repeat."

"Sex is not a necessity. Lust is a hormonal need, one that can be controlled."

"Your friends don't seem to control it."

"They're soldier models."

"And? What difference does that make?"

"Their testosterone levels are much higher, intentionally so. From what information I've gleaned over the years, human researchers noted early on in their studies that soldiers with higher levels of hormones were more efficient in combat. Better, more violent killers, in other words. In order to exploit this aspect, most of the cyborg units are programmed to create more testosterone than a normal male."

"Why does it not surprise me that the military would do something like that? Haven't you been able to dial it back?"

"If you mean reduce, we've tried. But, we can't completely eliminate it. Nor did most of the males want us to. So long as they can control their tempers and channel the violence, they are allowed to choose how they live."

"Choice?" She rolled the word off her tongue, mulling it. "What an interesting concept."

"It's more than a concept to us. It's how we live. Why we fight. We want the choice to live as we choose, not as mindless machines or tools for others."

"And you've achieved this on this world you've carved out for yourself?"

"More or less. We do of course have laws, basic ones, like you shall not kill your cyborg brothers, or steal."

"Kind of like the original ten commandments."

"In a sense. We've adopted tenets, which we all abide by so that we can live in harmony. But other than those basic rules, we make our own fate."

"Make your own fate. I like that. But, if that's the case, then why are you in space still acting the part of techno geek?"

He smiled, a genuine grin that warmed her. "Because this is what I enjoy. What I'm good at. Just because I have my freedom doesn't mean I don't want to work. We all work. We have to if we want to survive. I am well aware of my limitation. I am no good at building things or engaging in combat. I am the first to admit I am socially awkward. I am, however, gifted when it comes to fixing things and deciphering technology, even adapting it to fit our evolving needs."

"So you play doctor and scientist because it's what you love, and Aramus is obviously good at giving orders," she replied wryly.

"That he is," Einstein replied, meeting her gaze with a conspiratorial smile.

"What about Seth? What's he good at?"

"Driving everyone a little crazy."

She laughed. "That sounds like something he'd say."

"Because it is. Seth is a spy model, built to blend in perfectly with the humans. He hides skills and hardware we can only imagine."

"Hides? You mean you don't know for sure what he's capable of? And yet you all seem to trust him."

"I do, at any rate, as do many others. I owe him my life. He's rescued me from more than one dangerous situation. He's actually rescued quite a few of the cyborgs, even those considered impossible to reach. Much as he'd like you to see him as a jokester, he's actually quite deadly, and dedicated to the cyborg liberation."

"An onion."

Confusion knit his brow. "I'm sorry? Did you just compare him to a root vegetable?"

"I did. An onion, as in a man of many layers."

Einstein snorted. "And who makes grown males cry. An apt comparison. I shall have to recall it."

Leaving aside her ribs, and barely touching upon her breasts—globes that ached for his hands to cup them—Einstein palpated the skin behind her ears.

"Interesting," he muttered.

"What is?" Other than the fact he could forgo groping her boobs, but get intrigued by her boring ears.

"I feel no sign of the port you mentioned. No indentation or ridge. If you hadn't told me of its existence, I would have never known it was there."

"It is. You can slice me open and take a peek if you'd like."

"Not necessary. I believe you. Besides, it would serve no purpose. I don't have a computer I can safely hook you up to. Even if I don't believe you harbor any hidden time bombs, I prefer to exercise caution. I will wait until we get back to my main lab. I have a computer that lacks both wireless connectivity and is apart from the mainframe. A safe machine, if you will, that I can use to explore your direct access without introducing any viruses to our mainframe." Einstein stepped back from her. "You may get up now."

"So I'm clean, charming?"

"As far as I can tell. You may clothe yourself."

"That's it? You barely touched me."

"Visually, I detected no anomalies or lumps beneath your skin."

"But you didn't really check my tits." She cupped them, enjoying how his gaze couldn't seem to move from her hands.

"I—Uh, the, um scan was able to ascertain nothing but fatty tissues in your mammary glands. No need for me to palpate."

No need except for the fact she would have enjoyed it. She sat up, the sheet hugging the top of her breasts, but leaving her shoulders bare. "You didn't do any probing, though."

Boy did that fluster him. He turned away quickly, idly shuffling the tools on his tray. "That seems unnecessarily intrusive."

"Then don't do it for science. Do it for fun."

"Excuse me?" He whirled with a confused expression marring his face.

"Come on, you can't tell me you wouldn't like to touch me there." She peeked at him coyly through her lashes.

"It wouldn't be appropriate."

"Screw appropriate. I think you should be thorough, charming." She inched the sheet up her thigh, exposing the skin, watching his riveted gaze, the evident desire thrumming through him feeding her own arousal. How she wanted him to throw off his standoffish demeanor and caress her. "Touch me," she demanded in a husky voice. "I won't mind. And I know you'd like it."

He shook his head. "No, thank you."

"Come on. I owe you for waking me up."

For some reason, this brought a rigidness to his muscles. "You owe me nothing. You are free now, Bonnie. Despite what the military expected, you do not have to offer yourself to me or anyone. Your body is your own."

Good to know. But it didn't change the fact she was strangely aroused by this reticent man. "Well, since the choice is mine, why can't I choose to ask you for sex?"

"Because."

"Because? That's not an answer, charming." She strode toward him, hips undulating, fascinated by the way he swallowed hard and held himself so tightly wound. Before she could reach out and touch him, he stumbled back.

"I'm needed on the bridge. Why don't you take some time to rest and when you wake, I can have someone show you the ship while I slumber." He said this all in a rush of words before practically running out the door. Heck, he almost slammed into the portal so quickly did he dash.

Way to make a girl feel good. *And leave me feeling horny.* But he'd be back. After all, this was his room. And when he did return, she'd be waiting.

Chapter Seven

Clear invitation or not, Einstein couldn't do it. Couldn't touch the skin she so temptingly displayed. But oh, how he wanted to.

No amount of logic could convince him he wouldn't enjoy it. His dick especially seemed interested in seeing what hid between her thighs. The fact he knew all the biological details of the female body didn't seem to sway it from the senseless logic that somehow Bonnie's sexual organ would feel different from the one time he'd attempted intercourse with a sexbot.

It was only his rigid moral code—and irrational terror—that saved him from finding out first hand. Avoidance seemed the best plan of action, and he did his best to stick to this course, not an easy task given he shared his quarters with her. Over the next few days, he did his best to come to grips with the need she engendered. The desire. He took to hiding out in the gym and when she found him there and insisted they spar, pinning him more than once to the mat with a triumphant grin when he just couldn't bring himself to block her, he almost gave in to his baser human urges.

He found a new hiding spot in the engine room, but the cyborgs there ribbed him about his "girlfriend" and gave him up when she came looking. Heck, even Seth ridiculed him, using their mental communicator to call him a "chicken," and "an idiot for not eating the cake." What did food have to do with it?

Worst thing was, no matter how much he tried to avoid Bonnie, how he hid and ignored, she didn't take offense, just smiled and jested, "You can't run forever, charming."

How he hated the fact she was right. He quickly ran out of spots to hide from the female determined to tempt him. The willpower to resist eroded daily as she kept throwing herself in his path. Teasing him. Taunting him. Driving him senseless until all he could think of was her. Bonnie, a name he now held synonymous with seductress.

Sharing a room with her meant fighting his base human urges at every turn. He tried to time it so he arrived after she left, the computer notifying him whenever she exited to entertain herself elsewhere. He'd sneak in for a shower, and come out to find her lounging on his bed smirking. He'd lay down for a rejuvenating nap and wake to find her snuggled against him, somehow not setting off his internal alarms, which should have frightened him, but instead made him file it as just another defect within himself that he needed to check on.

Everywhere he turned, there she was, and he knew it was just a matter of time before he lost the battle and did as she asked. Touched her as she demanded. How long could he honestly hope to fight her allure before he let himself give in to the sexual urges which seemed to have taken over his mental faculties?

After a few days of exhausting evasion, he couldn't recall the reasons why he shouldn't just give in and discover the pleasure she seemed intent on bestowing. The one thing he never expected, though, was how strongly he'd react when he came across someone who wanted the very thing he denied. Jealousy, an emotion he had a definition for but never understood, became very clear to him a few days after her arrival.

*

On the hunt for her elusive geeky prince, because teasing him was the most fun she'd ever had, Bonnie found herself waylaid in the hall.

"Hey gorgeous, feel like joining us for some fun?"

Bonnie held in a sigh as the cyborg male, still all too human at the core, propositioned her. Astro was his name. He worked in the engine room with his roommate Ralph. She'd seen him a time or two on her hunts for Einstein, but never really paid him much mind. He, on the other hand, displayed too much interest. Given how he blocked her path, it seemed he'd decided to act upon it.

It occurred to her to put him in his place—she did after all excel in most martial arts and submission moves—but, bored and a little sexually frustrated, she decided to first screw with him a bit.

"Us? As in a threesome?"

The cybernetic unit, handsome in a rough-hewn way, all craggy features and bulging muscles, smiled as he eyed her up and down. He licked his lips and nodded. "Ralph and I have a room with a cot down this way."

How romantic. "I usually prefer a more one-on-one encounter."

"So we'll take turns. Although, if you're the Bonnie the soldiers used to talk about back on the base, then the way I hear it, you used to handle more than two back in the day."

Lucky her, even years later in space, her reputation preceded her. Funny how it never occurred to any of the jerks that perhaps she'd never possessed a choice. That perhaps she'd done the things she had out of self-preservation or to protect the others, protect the ones less mentally able to handle it. Men always assumed because she didn't put up much of a fight that she wanted sex with them. Not really, but back then, while she'd not been given a choice and had to let them do as they pleased, now she called the shots. She knew she could call out to Seth or even the irritable Aramus, her voice keyed to the onboard computer, and they'd teach these cyborg boys not to bother her. Or she could teach them herself.

Just as she prepared to show the crude soldier how a lady liked to be treated, Einstein came flying around the corner, his face set in a tight mask of anger. How unusual, and sexy. But not as hot as the fist he threw before anyone could say a word.

Crack! The cyborg who'd called her an easy slut stumbled into the wall from the force of the blow. With more fighting skill than she would have credited, her geeky prince lay into Astro with several perfectly aimed punches and kicks. It did nothing to ease the fury on his face or temper the light blazing from his eyes. She could only gape in astonishment—and more than a touch of arousal.

"How." Whack. "Dare." Kick. "You." Punch. "Speak to her that way," Einstein shouted, enunciating each word with distinction. "No matter what her past or what the military made her do, Bonnie is a guest on our ship and a lady. As such, you will treat her with respect!"

"Yes, sir." The properly chastised cyborg spoke through a split and swollen lip and attempted a salute.

She bit her lip so as to not giggle. While she'd come to expect a lot of things from Einstein, violence and jealousy wasn't one of them.

Turning his back on the cyborg, her prince held out his hand. "Let's go, Bonnie."

Before she could ask where, Einstein grabbed a hold of her hand and stalked off, aggression delineating his slim build and making heat coil in her lower stomach. Such chivalry, heretofore unknown to her, totally blew her away—and turned her on. "Thanks," she said when he didn't seem inclined to speak.

"Don't thank me. You shouldn't have been subjected to such crass treatment in the first place."

"It's not entirely his fault. I never made a secret of the use the military had for me."

"It doesn't excuse his behavior. This is not how we comport ourselves. We are better than humans. We are above such base urges."

"Are you really?"

"What's that supposed to mean?" Einstein halted abruptly and fixed her with an unblinking stare.

Oh for fuck's sake. Tired of obtuseness, she got aggressive. He didn't resist when she shoved him back against the wall of the corridor and encroached on his space, however, she did note his heart rate, already ticking rapidly, increased another notch.

"I mean that attraction to the opposite sex is a natural thing."

His lips thinned into a tight line. "Are you excusing his behavior?"

"No. I'll admit, his proposal wasn't exactly subtle."

"Subtle? He asked you to join him for a gang bang with his buddy." Einstein's anger radiated from him in an almost palpable wave.

She absorbed the emotion, fed on it; the outrage for her, the chivalry, again for her, and at the core, the jealousy, because despite his claims he came to her defense out of honor, she recognized what it was truly about. *My geeky prince is staking a claim whether he knows it or not.* And she didn't mind that one bit. "Okay, he was a jerk who needs a few lessons from Seth on how to approach a girl, but that didn't mean you had to go all medieval on his ass."

"Oh, yes I did."

His dark pronouncement sent a shiver down her spine that owed nothing to a chill and everything with delight. "Okay, maybe you did, but, just so you know, I was more than capable of handling it myself. And before you say I shouldn't have to, the truth is I'm going to have to. He's not the first soldier who's going to hit on me and he's not the last. Anything with a dick between his legs is liable to do it. Some just do it more eloquently than others."

"Like Seth."

Her nose wrinkled. "Yeah, I don't know if I'd call him eloquent."

"But he knows how to compliment and flatter."

"In his own fashion. Yet, so do you."

She wondered if he realized how human he appeared in that moment with both his brows arching high. "Me? I think you're mistaken. I'm the last person you could accuse of flirting."

"Says the man who brings me treats. Who fashioned me a flower out of metal scraps and left it on a pillow. Who gave up his bed and privacy. Who tries to hide his attraction even though it's obvious."

"I—"

"Who stutters deliciously whenever he gets embarrassed." She laughed when he fell silent. "I know you like me, Einstein."

"Of course I do. I like all my fellow cyborgs."

"I mean like as in the way a boy likes a girl." To prove her point, she cupped him, the hardness of his cock a plentiful handful.

He sucked in an unnecessary breath. "I am simply reacting in a normal biological manner to an attractive member of the opposite sex—"

Silly man, he still tried to deny it. She knew just the way to shut him up, or at the very least, fry some of his circuits. "Has anyone ever told you that you analyze things too much? Analyze this." She pressed her mouth to his, tasting the lips she'd wondered about since her waking. It was better than she could have imagined. Heat, desire, and arousal rose in a tumultuous rush, bringing all her nerve endings alive, alive in a way she'd never imagined feeling again.

Under the sensual assault of her mouth, his lips parted, and she took full advantage, sliding her tongue into the recess to caress the edge of his teeth. He let his own tongue tentatively caress hers. When she moaned, he grew bolder, his hands moving from a hesitant spot on her waist down to her buttocks, gripping her and pulling her snug against his body, his erection hard against her belly.

She dug her fingers into his shoulders, lifting herself on tiptoe to get a better angle, wanting and needing him to get closer. Wanting more of him. Wanting…

A wolf whistle and a shouted, "Way to go, Einstein," from up the hall had him pushing her away and stumbling back. Eyes glowing, his lips swollen and looking deliciously disheveled, he regarded her with lingering arousal and panic. "I'm sorry."

"For what? I was the one who kissed you."

"I shouldn't have manhandled you like that in public."

"Then take me somewhere private. I enjoyed it, charming, in case you hadn't noticed."

"But—"

Bonnie was done with his excuses. Done with going to bed horny. She knew she wasn't good enough for Einstein in the long term. Knew they didn't have a future, not with the baggage she carried from her past. But dammit, she wanted his body. Wanted to forget, even if for just a few hours, that she was a tarnished princess who could never hope for a happily ever after. Selfish or not, she wanted Einstein. Now. "Enough already. I swear if you don't come back with me to your room right this very second and fuck me, I am going to scream."

"Why?"

"Because I am horny. Aroused. Going out of my mind with need."

"I'm sure there are other units better suited and more skilled to take care of that biological necessity than me."

Her eyes almost popped out of her head in astonishment. "Are you seriously suggesting I go to someone else?"

She could see the struggle in him and it made her wish she was just a little bit bigger so she could shake him. Did he really not grasp the fact she wanted him and no one else? Was he that unbelievably stupid?

He sighed and his shoulders slumped. "No. I don't want you to go to anyone else."

Then why did he keep refusing unless… "Is this because of my reputation?"

"What are you talking about?"

"Don't act stupid. You heard, Astro. I'm sure you've heard the rumors. It's not like I made it a secret. I was the military's whore. B785, the cyborg chick you went to if you needed a good time."

"Not by choice."

"But I didn't fight it as much as I should have. I don't blame you for rejecting me. Who wants a known slut in their bed? You deserve better." Her shoulders slumped as she let shame and discouragement, something she usually kept bottled, overwhelm her.

"I don't care about your past. We all did things we're not proud of. Things we did because we had to. Things we didn't have a choice in. That's not why I'm saying no."

"Then why are you?" She peeked at him and saw him scrubbing a hand through his hair.

"Because I'm afraid of not measuring up. I'm not good when it comes to connecting with people. I have almost no experience. I don't want to disappoint you."

What a pair they were. "You could never disappoint me."

"But—"

"Oh would you stop over-analyzing and just come with me." When it looked like he might speak again, make that argue, she grabbed his hand and yanked. "Now, charming."

"Aye, aye, ma'am."

She peered back to see a wan smile curling his lips. "Did you just call me ma'am?"

"Well, you are pretty bossy."

"But cute bossy, right?"

His smile widened. "Very."

A grin beamed forth, warming her from head to toe. "Well then, since you like orders from cute, bossy women, I demand you follow me back to your room and have sex with me." When he would have replied, she cut him off. "Don't even think about talking or I'll screw you right here in the hall."

He clamped his mouth shut, and he didn't pull away as she tugged him in the direction of his room. On the contrary, his pace kept up with her quick steps, until practically running, they made it to the privacy of his quarters.

Only once the door slid shut did his nervousness return. But she knew the cure for that. Pressing herself to him, she took his mouth in an aggressive kiss that left no room for speech, or thoughts, or doubt. She left them both only one choice—passion. A flaming need. An electrical sizzle that soon had them both panting and rubbing against each other. Their hands gripped and rubbed, stroking through clothing that suddenly chafed.

"Undress me," she murmured against his mouth.

"Are you sure?"

"Now, charming." She injected some force in to her words.

"Yes, ma'am."

Oh how he made that sound so sexy. With hands that trembled only slightly, he removed the jumpsuit she'd modified to fit her frame until she stood nude, never once breaking off their kiss. She wasted no time pressing her warm body against his still clothed one.

"Touch me, charming."

Hesitant at first, his cool fingers skimmed down the skin of her back to the top of her buttocks, then with a suddenness that surprised a gasp from her, he palmed her cheeks, pulling her tight against him. In a moment, she went from the one in charge to the one mewling in need.

She'd unleashed the man within, the passionate male who suddenly had his hands everywhere, stroking her skin and bringing nerve endings alive in a way she'd never thought to feel again. When he cupped her breasts for the first time, she tore her mouth from his as her head fell back and a long groan escaped her. "Yes," she hissed. "That's it. Squeeze them. Suck them."

He obeyed with a ravenous hunger, his mouth latching on to her nipples, inhaling them between his lips. The tug on her throbbing nubs sent a jolt right down to her moist pussy.

Fuck, how she ached for him. She reached between their bodies and unbuckled his pants, eager for her own chance to touch. He sprang into her hand, his cock hard and thick. His hips jerked as she stroked his length and he released her breast to utter an incoherent sound.

"Do you like that?" she asked in a husky voice.

He couldn't answer, but he did brace his hands on the wall, bracketing her, his hips thrusting in time to her strokes. A shudder went through him, then another. With a hoarse cry, he came, hot semen spilling over her hand and hitting her lower belly.

She uttered a pleased chuckle, but he froze and she peered up to see him looking horrified. "What's wrong, charming?" As soon as she said it, she knew though. He was a man, and he'd come before her. Never mind the fact he'd obviously needed it, men had this notion that woman always came first.

She, on the other hand, was glad he had. It would make the main event last longer.

"I'm sorry," he whispered, confirming her supposition.

"For what? Showing me how much I excite you?" She smiled as wide as she could. "That is the greatest compliment you could pay me, charming."

"But I didn't pleasure you. I failed."

"How did you fail? You don't really think we're done, do you?"

He looked down pointedly.

A delighted giggle escaped her. "Oh, charming. I am going to have so much fun teaching you." Starting now. Dropping to her knees, she brought herself eye level with his cock. He sucked in a breath at the first lick of the tip of his mushroom cap.

"What are you doing?" he said in a whisper.

Forget telling him, she showed him, and lucky her, he was a fast learner.

*

Einstein couldn't help himself from ejaculating. He tried and tried to hold back, but sexually repressed for so long, Bonnie hot and panting pressed against him, her hand gripping him so deliciously, he lost the battle.

Oh, the shame of it. The horror. The most intense pleasure he'd ever experienced quickly turned into humiliation. Even he knew a male should pleasure a female before himself. And he'd failed. Failed her. It was enough to make him want to self destruct. Or at least slink away so he wouldn't have to face her.

But Bonnie, his sweet princess, or so he now thought of her, not that he'd ever say so aloud, forgave him, even seemed pleased by his lack of control. To his shock, she took his selfish act as a compliment and then proceeded to thank him for it by dropping to her knees and showing him exactly why males talked with reverence about the 'til now mysterious joys of a blowjob.

By all the circuitry in his head, just about every nanobot in his body fried when her lips gripped his cock in a tight suction. Illogical or not, the sensation of her mouth working up and down the length of his dick felt unbelievably good. Better than good, it was…indescribable. Perfect. Decadent.

And as she'd promised, they were far from done. His cock came back bigger and harder than before. His desire roared through him, a hot electrical current that brought all his organic senses alive, but this time, he kept better control and he remembered some of the things he'd learned about sex.

However, the dry teachings in his head needed actual experimentation. Hands-on treatment. Tongue on cleft. In other words, Einstein wanted to experience it for himself—in the name of research, of course.

Oh who was he kidding? He hungered in a way logic couldn't explain for Bonnie.

Good as her mouth felt on his cock, he tugged himself free and drew her up. Her bright eyes questioned him and her full lips opened to speak, but he didn't wait to hear. Dropping to his knees as she'd done, he spread her labia with his now warm fingers to expose the nub hidden within. He put the knowledge in his head to use and tongued her.

"Oh, charming," she sighed at the first stroke, but that was the last coherent thing she said as he did to her what she did to him. He feasted on her. Licking, sucking, and exploring her pussy, he couldn't believe he'd denied them both this pleasure. How exquisite she tasted. How fascinating her reactions. How unbelievably erotic and stimulating it proved to caress her flesh with his mouth. She tugged at his hair, encouraging him, and he grew bolder, probing her sex with his tongue. But it wasn't enough. He inserted a digit and was shocked at the heat of her. The moistness. The strength with which the muscles of her channel gripped him. He wondered how it would feel to sink his dick into the haven of her sex, to have it grip him.

It seemed she wanted to know as well because she gasped, "Fuck me. Give me that big cock of yours, charming. I want to feel you inside me."

That made two of them. Standing, he only needed to lift her a little to align her with his shaft. Her legs wrapped around his waist, drawing his swollen member to the mouth of her sex, the tip of him wedging at the entrance. He held back from thrusting as fast and hard as he longed to, worried about causing her discomfort. She wasn't in the mood to take things slow, though. Locking her legs around him, she yanked and forced him into her.

Oh. My. God. He'd never believed in a deity or heaven until that moment. A thousand sensations exploded at once on his already overburdened senses. Mindless with pleasure, his body nevertheless understood what it needed, what she wanted. In and out he thrust, each stroke causing her muscles to tighten around him, increasing the bliss, building the pressure.

She began to chant, "Yes! Yes! Harder, charming. Harder." He obeyed her, increasing his tempo, pumping deep as she clawed at his shoulders until she sobbed his name and came with a decibel-shattering shriek.

The convulsive wave that went through her body as she climaxed swept him along in its wake. His cock pulsed then exploded, joining her in ecstatic bliss.

It left them both panting and sweating, their bodies intimately intertwined. For the first time that he truly recalled, Einstein finally felt *alive*. He hugged Bonnie to him and rested his cheek on the top of her head. He closed his eyes as he basked in the sensation.

Now he understood why so many of his brothers enjoyed sex. Why some of his brethren chose to settle down with one woman. Why the ballads and stories of love and romance existed.

He didn't even have the words to explain or express the tumultuous feelings he went through there were so many. Bonnie, though, summed it up best. "Wow, that was fun."

Simply put, but apt. Einstein chuckled. "Yes. Yes, it was."

"Want to do it again?"

As a matter of fact, he did. Several times.

Chapter Eight

After a night spent in Bonnie's arms, Einstein revised his stance on sex. Actually, he pretty much erased all his previous erroneous suppositions. Sex was good. Great. Incredible. Totally necessary and addictive. He'd lost count of the number of times he and Bonnie indulged. Okay, not true, he'd ejaculated four times while she'd reached an orgasmic state six times, having the advantage of quick regeneration.

Even better, with sex out of the way, he finally felt at ease with himself again. More in control. Relaxed. It figured his friends would notice.

Glancing up from his console, Seth said a brief hello before looking down again. Barely a second passed before his head snapped back up and his eyes widened. "Holy shit. I don't believe it. Einstein finally got a piece."

"A piece of what?" Aramus asked absentmindedly as he pored over some data.

"A great big piece of ass with a side dish of the cat who ate the canary. Way to go, dude." Seth held up his hand for a high-five, which Einstein ignored, but he couldn't control the blush that heated his cheeks. Was his self-satisfaction that evident?

Apparently it was because Aramus peered at him and grunted. "About time. Maybe now you can concentrate on why these numbers look off."

Did Aramus accuse him of missing something? "Off? What do you mean off?" Indignant, Einstein slid into his seat and perused the data Aramus pointed out. He noted the anomaly right away and wanted to groan at his obvious mental incapacity. "I'm sorry. I should have noted this."

"I'm sure you would have if your head had been in the game instead of buried in some sweet pussy."

"Can we not talk about that?" Einstein stammered. "We've got more important things to discuss."

"Fine, dude. You can give me the details later, unless you videotaped it?" At Einstein's glare, Seth sighed. "You are still no fun. So other than sex, what's got both your panties in a twist?" Seth asked, leaning over to glance at the screen.

"According to these readings, there's some activity on the seventh asteroid circling this galaxy's sun."

"Is this the same asteroid we were supposed to mine in this sector?"

"No. But it's close."

"I take it that what you're detecting isn't from one of our crews?"

"None that we authorized and it wasn't there the last time we came through," Aramus added.

"What do you think it is?" Seth asked.

"Could be pirates," Einstein mused. "They're always relocating their bases to keep out of reach of the space authorities. And the minerals on the surface are thick and rich enough to tempt them if they're willing to put in a bit of work."

"Which seems unlikely. The smugglers I know prefer to steal than do actual labor. Perhaps a mining company has set up a new camp?"

"Or it could be a new military hideout," Aramus announced with a predatory gleam in his eye. "Whatever it is, we should check it out."

"Are you forgetting something?" Einstein said.

A groan left Aramus. "Stupid female. Ruining my fun again."

"We have our orders," Einstein reminded. Poor Aramus. Their orders from Joe were clear. No taking any chances with their passenger, which meant no side trips to check out anomalies.

"Whatever it is, we'll have to check it out with our next pass through this space."

"Check what out?" Bonnie's sudden appearance brought a smile to Einstein's lips.

Appearing freshly showered and more beautiful than ever, she sauntered into the command center and plopped herself on his lap as if she owned it. And after last night, as far as Einstein was concerned, she did. Of course, her public display meant he needed to ignore Aramus' growl of annoyance and Seth's chortle, but her curvy frame made the task easy. "Good morning, Bonnie."

A smile curved her lips. "It definitely is, charming. I hope you don't mind me visiting."

"Do we have a choice?" Aramus mumbled. "It's not like you listen to anything I say."

"Oh, Aramus. Admit it, you love having me around."

"Like a rusty bolt under my skin."

Einstein hid a grin at their bantering. In the past few days of travel, when she wasn't hunting him down, Bonnie seemed to enjoy driving Aramus insane. It amused Seth to no end, and oddly enough, despite his bellowing and grumbling, Einstein suspected Aramus enjoyed the word play too.

"Now, now children," Seth chided, humor in his tone. "This isn't the time for schoolyard taunts. Save them for later. We have actual have work to do."

"Oh. Is something the matter?" Bonnie asked, her expression turning serious.

Einstein replied. "We found some suspicious readings on a nearby asteroid and are noting it so the next team out can check on it."

"Sounds like fun. But why wait?"

"We've got orders to go avoid any possible complications."

"So you're just going to ignore it? What if it's not there when you come back? What if it's important?"

"She raises good points," Aramus grunted.

"It could be dangerous," Einstein pointed out.

"Why? Are we going to have to fight?"

"We don't know what it is yet. It could be nothing."

"Then, why ignore it?" Einstein gave her a pointed look. "Oh. *Oh.*" Understanding dawned and she frowned. "Well, that's just dumb. You can't pretend it's not there just because you've got me onboard. Surely it wouldn't hurt to take a closer peek."

"She does raise a good point," Aramus replied slowly. "If we're careful, we could get in closer and get a better idea of what we're seeing. This ship is equipped with the latest technology when it comes to hiding from radar."

"Einstein created his own version of a cloaking device," Seth chimed in. "The man's a bloody genius."

"Not really." Einstein just liked tinkering with things until they did what he wanted.

"And he's too modest."

"So I've noticed," Bonnie replied with a small laugh. "If we're hidden from possible enemy eyes, then what can it hurt? I say you check it out."

"Joe won't like it."

"Joe's not here."

"And we could use those minerals."

Bonnie clapped her hands. "It's decided then. What can I do to help?"

"You? Help?" Aramus chuckled, his disdain for her abilities clear.

Einstein shot him a dirty look. "Why don't you let her tell us what she can do before making fun of her?"

"Or else what, brainiac?"

"Or else I'll reprogram you to do the chicken dance. I hear it was quite popular back on earth."

The big cyborg's eyes narrowed. "You wouldn't dare."

"Keep treating her the way you do and you'll soon see," Einstein snapped back.

For some reason, Seth found his threat immensely funny and couldn't stop laughing.

To her credit, Bonnie didn't laugh, but she did squirm, distracting him. "Boys, no need to get all nasty with each other. Aramus, in his usual delicate manner, asked a valid question. I've never really told you what I am capable of."

"Other than distracting my crew."

"That's a natural talent," she retorted. "But not my primary purpose. I'm actually a graduate of advanced communications and excellent decoder of cyphers. There isn't a scrambled message I can't figure out."

"Bullshit."

Einstein flipped his middle finger at his commander for his foul expletive, which sent Seth into even greater hysterics, probably because it was so out of character. However, captain of this vessel or not, Einstein discovered he didn't like the disparaging way Aramus treated Bonnie—even if half of the time she encouraged it. As her prince, he owed it to her to protect her. Ugh, since when did he succumb to the fairy tale idea she kept spouting? Probably since he enjoyed the fact she thought him her prince. He'd never been someone's hero before.

"Laugh all you want, grumpy one. It's the truth. Inside this cute bod hides the greatest puzzle solver the military could create. They embedded the ability into my internal cortex before realizing the effect it would have on my programming. The scientists hypothesized that my ability to see through codes is what made their attempts to control me fail. My mind saw right through it and ignored it."

"Cool." Seth uttered the word with reverence. "Wish I'd gotten me some of that. It would have come in handy on a few missions and when I try to do the *Sunday Times* crossword."

"And here we thought you just downloaded the newspaper for the cartoons."

"Ouch!" Seth replied, chuckling at Aramus' barb.

"What's your success rate with foreign coding?"

"I wouldn't know. They never let me off the base. Apparently, since they couldn't leash me, they deemed me a threat to security. How right they were."

Einstein couldn't help but grin at her pleased expression. "Well, we don't have any targets yet, and we've yet to intercept any communications. However, knowing we've got a master decoder might come in handy. I've got some skill in that area, but I'll admit I'm more of a scientific puzzler than a message one."

"If you're done jabbering, can we get back to the asteroid?" Aramus interrupted. "If it's pirates, they might have some supplies we can pilfer."

"Woohoo. Raid." Seth practically bounced in his seat.

"Or it might be nothing," Einstein admonished. "It wouldn't be the first time signals got caught and bounced around, making it appear as if there's something there when there isn't."

"How come no one ever mentions the possibility of aliens?" Bonnie asked with an innocence Einstein thought cute—but illogical.

"The chances of encountering sentient life are astronomical. Considering how far we've traveled and the technology we have access to, if other life forms existed, we'd have seen a sign by now."

She made a moue of disappointment. "Bummer. So it's either pirates, miners, or ghost space chatter."

"Could be the military too. Why don't you hang out while we swing in for a closer peek?"

"Awesome."

"Excuse me, lovebirds, but as the captain, isn't that my call?" Aramus interjected.

"May I watch, oh mighty commander?" Bonnie turned in Einstein's lap and batted her lashes at Aramus. Einstein stifled a laugh, as did Seth. "Pretty please with a great big cherry bomb filled with all kinds of yummy explosives inside?"

Even their gruff leader couldn't say no. "Fine. You can stay. But no getting in the way. And that means no kissing and cuddling. This is after all the command center, not some make-out room."

"Thank you," she squealed, hopping up and giving Aramus a sassy salute. "I'll be good. Promise. Besides, I need to recuperate after last night. Who knew charming was such an animal in the bedroom."

Forehead, meet console. Groaning at her announcement, Einstein did his best to ignore the laughter and concentrate, but inside, he smiled. Cyborg or not, the human part of him enjoyed the compliment and looked forward to a repeat performance. First things first, though. They had an asteroid to check out.

Slowing their speed in order to engage the semi-cloaking device he'd created that masked the signs of their approach, they swung in closer to the large rock drawing their interest. Less than two miles across, it revolved in a steady orbit around the oversized star, which acted as a sun for this particular part of space. Initial scans didn't show much of interest. The metals embedded in the surface of low or sparse density, not worth the

119

effort to mine. Scrap the idea of a mining installation. And he also vetoed the ghost chatter theory as the low level signal emanating from the inside the asteroid became more distinct.

"It's definitely human chatter," Einstein announced when he managed to clear out the static muffling the frequency. "Slang speech. Mostly of a personal nature. Analysis shows less than a point zero zero three chance that it's military in nature.

"Yay. Pirates." Seth fist pumped. "Please tell me we can raid them for some stuff. I'd love a chance to exercise."

Drumming his fingers on his armrest, Aramus didn't immediately reply. His brows drew together. "I don't know. It's not part of our mission itinerary."

"But it could net us some cool booty."

"There's a chance of casualty." Snickers met Aramus' announcement and he recanted with a chuckle. "Okay, casualty to them. But you know what Joe would say seeing as how we've got one of the females onboard."

Einstein did know and agreed. Given their rarity, they shouldn't undertake anything that might jeopardize her. Still, though, a handful of pirates against a squadron of cyborgs?

"What? You're going to cancel what should be a cake walk because of me? That's ridiculous." Bonnie didn't bother to couch her words.

"I know. Especially since you won't be anywhere near the action."

"What? That's no fair. If you're going treasure hunting, I want to go to." Her lower lip jutted.

Einstein's might have been the most vehement "No!" but it wasn't alone.

Aramus shook his head. "Sorry, PITA. If I agree to let us swing in for a raid, then you're staying here where it's safe. I am not going to be the one who has to tell Chloe I let her sister get killed because I lacked the balls to make her stay behind."

"Not to mention what Joe will do to us if we make Chloe cry." Seth shuddered. "The man is irrational when it comes to his woman."

A feeling Einstein could now relate to better since he'd met Bonnie. To what lengths would he go to in order to keep her safe?

"You guys are no fun." She pouted.

"Would it help if we said we'll bring you back a treat?" Seth offered.

"It better be a chocolate bar. I've been dying for one since I woke up."

"We'll do our best," he promised.

Shooting Seth a dark look, Einstein controlled himself before he said something illogical—and jealous—such as, "If anyone brings her a present, it will be me." He had a better plan. Find something chocolate or sweet first. Or in the worst case, if Seth did, steal it from him and present it as his own prize.

Preparing didn't take long. They'd gone on mini missions as a unit so many times they knew the steps by rote. For Bonnie, though, this was a first. Just before he boarded the small craft that would take them to the surface of the asteroid along with a few other crew members, she threw her arms around him and hugged him tight.

In his ear she whispered, "Please come back to me in one piece. I couldn't bear to lose you now."

What should a cyborg new to relationships answer? "Our probability of success is ninety-seven percent." His dry statistic made her chuckle.

"Oh, charming. You say the most senseless things, but I like you anyway." She sealed her statement with a kiss that left his lips tingling. Bemused, he took his spot in the cruiser and ignored the jibes of his unit.

She said she likes me. And despite his theory on emotions being a biological imbalance, he couldn't help but think, *awesome, because I like her too.*

Chapter Nine

Being banned from the action sucked. Bored, Bonnie swung her legs over the armrest of the commanding chair and ignored the dirty look from Aphelion left behind to monitor the ship and surface—AKA to babysit her.

"Are they there yet?" she asked, twirling a strand of hair.

"No."

"You didn't even check."

"Because you asked less than three minutes and fifteen seconds ago. The answer remains the same."

"You know, for a guy with a cool name, you're a real tight ass."

"A steady regimen in the gym would help you achieve the same posterior musculature."

Great. Another cyborg who took everything literally. However, unlike Einstein, she didn't find it cute at all. Gone only for an hour and she missed him already, which really didn't bode well. Yes, she'd chased after him, determined to get him into bed. Mostly because she liked the challenge he posed. The more he resisted, the more she just had to have him. And only him.

For some reason, he got her motor running, almost quite literally. Something about him totally turned her on. His shy smiles. His courteous manner. His intelligence. His looks. His bod. There wasn't a damned thing about him she didn't like. And when she finally got him right where she wanted him? Between her thighs, making her scream and pant with delight. Pure, orgasmic rapture. And absolute disaster.

Already she could tell he was forming an attachment to her. Liked her. And oh how she liked him. A lot. But despite his claim that her past didn't matter, she knew better. Sure, he said the fact she used to be the military slut didn't bother him, but a guy like him deserved better than her. He was too good and kind to end up with a girl with a reputation no one would ever forget, least of all her. However, Bonnie, still selfish it seemed even after everything she'd gone through, couldn't help but wish otherwise. Couldn't help but want the happily ever after other women dreamed of. *I can't help but want my prince charming.*

And for now, she'd have him. They had a few weeks left to enjoy before they hit the cyborg homeworld and she intended to make the most of them. To enjoy her geeky prince. To teach him the confidence she knew he possessed so that when she ended their affair and walked away—crying internal tears—he'd find the right girl to settle down with. Someone who wouldn't embarrass him with her past. As for her…well, she'd do as she always had. Swallow her pain and go on. At least she wouldn't be alone, though. Chloe would be there. Not that she intended to lean on her sister too much. Chloe didn't need Bonnie fucking things up for her, not when she'd finally gotten the love she deserved.

Fuck, did it hurt and depress her to think about doing the right thing. No wonder most people took the easy route. Being good sucked. Just like waiting.

She sighed and drummed her fingers on the armrest, flicking switches back and forth, back and forth.

"Aramus doesn't like people touching the controls," Aphelion stated for the millionth time.

"Aramus can kiss my mechanically enhanced ass," she retorted. "You and I both know he locked down the controls on his seat before he left. The big man knew I'd be sitting here. Who wouldn't? Those little bucket seats are damned uncomfortable."

"Comfort is not a requirement when on a mission."

A moue of annoyance curled her lips. "Maybe not, but it sure would help when someone gets left behind. I don't get it. What's taking them so long? I thought this was supposed to be a quick raid and grab."

"They've been gone less than an hour. Hardly long. It's not like they could go through the front bay doors. According to their schedule, they should have docked on the far side of the asteroid about thirty minutes ago."

"Or so we assume. This whole not running surface scans so we don't give ourselves away thing really bites the big one." Especially since it meant she couldn't keep close tabs on her prince.

"Mission protocol dictates—"

"Oh would you shove it with your damned mission protocol? I'm worried. Would it kill you to have a little compassion? You know, that human emotion that allows you to feel empathy for the anxiety another sentient being is going through when someone she cares about is doing something dangerous." Without her.

Aphelion appeared to ponder her words because his reply emerged in a gentler, less formal tone. "I am sure the deployed units are fine. They've taken every precaution. They even dressed in anti-gravity suits to reduce the stress on their bodies."

"You really think they're okay?"

"I know they are," he stated with certainty. "We just need to—"

"Wait. I know." She sighed. Patience, not something she'd possessed much of when completely human and still didn't as a cyborg. "You know, I always expected missions to be more exciting than this. In the movies, the heroes ram through the main doors, blasting everything in their path. They kill all the bad guys in a wicked gun fight, get the treasure, and save the girl."

Aphelion snorted, her words finally drawing a human reaction. "In real life, the chances of such a haphazard plan succeeding are slim. Not to mention the unnecessary damage they'd sustain. Properly executed missions follow a subversive path. The less violence involved the more chances of them prevailing and returning without casualty."

"I still don't see why they had to take Einstein with them. I thought he was the brains of the operation. Shouldn't he be here, I don't know, doing brainy stuff with the computers like taking over their surveillance system and making their computers do funky things such as lock the pirates in their rooms? Or have their own weapons turn on them?"

"Your practical knowledge of actual missions is appalling. Might I suggest you study something other than violence glorifying movies with unrealistic storylines and instead try something a little more cerebral like *The Art of War*?"

"Anyone ever tell you that you're a killjoy?"

"And you are incredibly uninformed considering the fact you're a cyborg."

"Way to insult me, Aphelion."

"I apologize. It wasn't my intent."

"Don't be sorry. I asked for it. And guess what? Stick in the mud or not, I think I'm starting to like you."

"I'd prefer if you didn't. I saw what you liking Einstein did to him."

She sighed happily. "Yeah, he is so cute when frazzled."

His only reply resembled a snort, which was a step up from disdain, in her mind. *I am totally winning him over.* Aphelion returned to studying his

127

console and she continued to wait for any kind of word.

Despite her boredom, Bonnie didn't stray too far from the main control area, not wanting to miss anything, especially not once the action, or inaction started.

She'd partially dozed off, her BCI powering down to save energy, when Aphelion shuffled in his seat with a muttered, "Well, this is odd."

Straightening, she asked, "What is?"

"All the chatter on the asteroid's communications network just went dead."

"Are you sure they didn't change frequency?"

"First thing I checked. There's nothing on any of the bands."

"Let me see." Bonnie hopped up and peered over his shoulder, frowning. "That is odd. Do you think the pirates know the boys are coming?"

"If they did, we should have seen an increase in radio activity, not a decrease."

While his fingers tapped away, Bonnie wandered to another console and she pulled up some more data, widening the search parameters to include not just signals bouncing around the asteroid, but from the other asteroids nearby. Nothing appeared; however, her gut, a leftover human presentiment that she couldn't ignore, said something didn't add up. Illogical, her BCI claimed.

Perhaps the asteroid entered a sleep cycle. Or a generator went down. The audio blackout could have a valid explanation. But her instincts screamed something was wrong. *Einstein's in danger.*

"Can you pull up the recordings of their chatter for the last few hours?" she asked seating herself in the bucket seat beside Aphelion.

"Sure. But there's nothing there. Just dull space chatter about breakfast and who's exchanging sexual favors with each other. Regular human stuff."

"It doesn't hurt to look again." Putting on a head set, she closed her eyes to better concentrate on the voices and the words the ship recorded. Splitting them out into distinct streams, she ordered her BCI to analyze the seeming innocuous communications. On the third pass, she caught the pattern. Opening her eyes, she barked out, "Holy shit. It's a trap!"

"What? How can you tell that? We haven't heard or seen anything to suggest such a scenario." Aphelion didn't bother to hide his skepticism.

"We didn't hear a thing because we were listening to the surface and not looking deeper. Just like *they* wanted."

"And who's *they*?"

"It's not fucking pirates with contraband down there, it's the bloody military. This whole installation is a setup, a decoy meant to draw in raiders or cyborgs. They don't care which."

"So the units will have to fight a little harder."

"A little harder?" A bitter laugh escaped her. "I don't think you're grasping the severity. The soldiers down there are equipped with the latest in weaponry. Or so the code I deciphered states. They know we're onto them. They know we're not pirates, they just aren't sure if we're human or not. They've armed the soldiers with electrical stun guns, the new ones Seth was telling me about that can lay a cyborg male flat, long enough for them to disable them." AKA kill because the military no longer took cyborgs prisoner.

A stricken expression crossed Aphelion's face. "Perhaps you're mistaken."

"I wish. We have to do something."

"We can't. We have our orders. We're to maintain orbit around this moon and stay out of sight until rendezvous."

"But that was before we knew they were walking into an ambush. We can't just sit here and let them get killed."

"And what do you expect me to do?"

"Contact them."

"I'll try."

She tried not to grind her teeth as he closed his eyes and did the mind-to-mind talking thing the male cyborgs could do. His brow creased. "They're not replying. I think they've shut off their communicators."

"Or something is jamming them," she replied grimly.

"We shall have to hope the units catch on to the ruse."

"Not good enough."

"What else do you expect me to do? I cannot contact them."

"Then there's only one option left."

"And that is?"

"We need to rescue them, of course."

"Of course, because that's so easy," he drawled, his sarcasm thick. "You do realize it took them over an hour to get to the hidden installation."

"Because they were going in the back door, undercover. We can make it there in, what, twenty, fifteen minutes if we really push this baby."

"Are you suggesting we attack the facility?"

"Yes."

He gaped at her for a moment. "Do you need to shut down and perform a full system reboot?"

"Is this your way of calling me crazy?"

"As a matter of fact, it is. That is the most insane thing you've uttered so far."

"I'm not crazy, nor mentally deficient or unstable. Nor do I need to reboot. However, you need a mental tweaking of your BCI, though, if you don't see something wrong with letting friends and fellow cyborgs walk knowingly into a trap. Maybe you can live with yourself knowing you're sentencing them to death, but I can't. Orders or not, I am going to do something to help them."

"This is mutiny."

"No, it's called doing what's right and saving my friends." And saving her prince charming.

"Aramus won't like it."

"Aramus can kiss my heart-shaped ass right after I save his. Now are you going to help me or not?"

Aphelion sighed. "Much as a part of me is arguing against it, oddly enough, I also find myself in agreement. So what do you propose we do?"

"Make our presence known and distract them long enough that our boys can get out."

"I'll need a minute to unlock the controls of the ship."

Smirking, Bonnie plopped herself in Aramus' seat and let her fingers fly. "Already done, or did you really think all that switch flipping was random?" As if Aramus' passwords could keep her out. "Hang on tight, Aphelion. We are about to go knocking on the military's door."

And save her prince charming.

Chapter Ten

"Surrender now and you won't be harmed." The order came through the speakers embedded at intervals in the wall and the cyborgs sneaking along the suspiciously empty polymer corridor halted in their tracks.

"Are they talking to us, do you think?" Seth whispered. They didn't dare communicate mind-to-mind lest the wireless signal give them away.

"We didn't trip any alarms," Einstein replied.

"So you assume," Aramus rumbled.

"So I know. I've been checking. There was nothing along this path that would have triggered a warning to let them know we're coming," Einstein argued.

"Nothing? Really? Then how the fuck did they detect us? I thought this place was equipped with only the barest surveillance?" Aramus growled.

Einstein tapped on his handheld tablet and frowned. "It is. I mean, we're talking really low level stuff. I don't get it."

"Maybe they're fishing. Or talking to someone else. Do you think group B was detected?" Seth interjected.

"Unlikely." Einstein had sent the second group of cyborgs through a natural fissure in the rock he discovered on his scans to flank the opposite side. According to his calculations, they shouldn't yet have reached the point where they needed to laser their way in, nor should they have encountered any security cameras.

"Then maybe it's another group of pirates come to steal."

Both Einstein and Aramus shot Seth an incredulous look. As if two raiding parties chose the same moment to sneak in. The next announcement laid that ill-thought theory to rest.

"We have you surrounded, cyborgs. Give up peacefully and you will be given a chance to serve again with new and improved programming."

Un-fucking believable. Not often prone to foul language, the moment called for it even if the expletive never passed Einstein's lips. He and his friends exchanged stunned looks.

"Um, I'd say that answers the question of if they know we're here." Hooray for Seth, king of stating the obvious.

"Yeah and is it me, or did anyone notice they didn't sound like bloody pirates?"

"Probably because it's the military." A disturbing realization. *How did I miss that important fact when I reconnoitered this seemingly harmless outpost?* "They set a trap for us. And I missed it. Sorry."

"Fuck me. The military outsmarted our smartest cyborg." Aramus groaned. "What is my world coming to when humans are smarter than machines?"

"Oh stop being such a drama queen," Seth cajoled with a poke in their leader's ribs. "Who would have expected it, especially way out here? The military isn't usually known for its subtlety."

"We'll have to investigate this change in their tactics later." And reprogram their protocols to take this new furtiveness into account for future missions. At the moment, they had more pressing issues. "What should we do? If the military planned this ambush, then chances are there are no supplies for us to acquire."

"Not exactly. They will have weapons. Maybe even a ship or two. And who knows, maybe this wasn't a trap, but an actual hidden outpost we stumbled upon. We won't know what they have unless we keep exploring."

"They're not just going to hand those things to us. Not without a fight."

"So what do you suggest? Tucking our tails and running like cowards?" Aramus drawled.

The odds on retreating and making it back to their hidden transport vessel intact seemed slim, especially with their presence discovered. Einstein ran a few scenarios in his head and couldn't come to any solution that didn't involve a battle with the humans. Not to mention, a retreat to their hopefully hidden ship meant leading them back to Bonnie. Put her in danger or battle it out? Einstein knew what he would choose.

Aramus came to the same conclusion. "I say we fight." He cracked his knuckles and rolled his head on his neck, limbering up his enhanced musculature. A predatory light illuminated his eyes. "We can't retreat. So our best option is to go forward and take them out."

"Excellent. I was hoping you'd say that." Seth pulled a pair of slim blades from his sleeves. "I could use some real exercise."

"Bet you I bag more kills," Aramus taunted.

"In your dreams, you inferior model."

Einstein groaned. "Why is it none of the missions I ever go on with you two ever end up simple?"

"Because we're magnets for fun, dude."

Fun if bloodshed counted. "Should we warn the units approaching from the other side?"

Aramus shook his head. "We don't yet know which of our groups they've detected. If we have a chance at surprising them, we should keep it."

"What about our ship?" And Bonnie. Was she safe or did the military at this very moment surround them and demand their surrender? He almost broke radio silence to find out.

"If it looks like we're not going to make it out, we'll send a signal for them to retreat."

"We'll win," Seth said with quiet assurance.

"What makes you so sure?" Einstein asked. Worry tainted his query as for the first time in awhile he recognized his own mortality, probably because now he had something, make that someone, to live for.

"We'll win because I am too young and handsome to die." Seth laughed. "Oh come on. Lighten up, brainiac. This is what we were made for. What we excel at. We are fighting machines. Deadly soldiers. The best of the best. Humans don't stand a chance against us."

"Says the man equipped with both guns and knives. Not all of us are as well trained," Einstein remarked dryly.

"Are you calling me a crappy teacher?" Seth adopted a hurt expression.

"No. But you know I'm more adept with a keyboard than my fists."

"Practice makes perfect. And just think, when you return victorious to the ship, you'll have someone to fawn over you and kiss your booboos better."

He did, didn't he? Einstein straightened. And Bonnie hated the military. She'd probably see his fighting as heroic. "I like your logic. What are we waiting for?"

In the distance, they heard the crackle of gunfire. Nobody needed to state the obvious aloud. Group B had encountered resistance.

Forget coming at the waiting soldiers with subtlety. With a wide, ferocious grin, Aramus pulled a gun, and with his other hand holding a deadly knife, pointed it forward. "Ready? Cyborgs attack!"

And with that savage, rallying cry, they took off at a run, exhilaration and nano-imbued blood coursing through their veins. For once, Seth had it right. This was what cyborgs were created for. Perfect killing machines. Impervious to pain. Almost indestructible. And oh so deadly.

Humanity's greatest achievement, and biggest failure, ready to mete justice on their creators.

Chapter Eleven

Bonnie didn't have a clue what to expect once she convinced Aphelion they needed to charge in to the rescue. She'd never actually flown a spacecraft before or engaged in a real battle. All her knowledge came from lessons programmed into her BCI and from the movies she recalled. However, she didn't let a pesky thing like inexperience stop her.

Einstein and the others needed their help, and damn it all, she was going to deliver. Thankfully, Aphelion seemed to have some knowledge of what needed to happen. The ship hummed as it went into motion, and a peek at the screens showed them heading toward the asteroid and not away like she initially feared. With half the crew invading the fake installation, and the other half still on board, they'd have to work in concert to pull this off. Good thing cyborgs excelled at teamwork. The few cyborgs left aboard didn't show up to ask them what the hell was going on, although she could tell by the line between Aphelion's eyes that they did contact him on a neural level. She didn't hear those conversations, but when she saw his shoulders relax, she assumed everyone agreed with her half-assed plan.

And what was that plan? Oh yeah, somehow get close enough to the asteroid to draw the military's attention away from Einstein and the group of cyborgs about to walk into a trap. What she furiously tried to figure out what how to do that without blasting the damned place to bits, which would kind of defeat the purpose.

"So, um, Aphelion?"

"Yes."

"I don't suppose you have any ideas on what we should do once we reach the asteroid?"

Fingers never pausing their furious tapping on his control panel, he nevertheless rotated his head and gazed at her, the first hints of mirth curling the corners of his lips. "Who, me? This is your mutiny. I thought the plan was to go in guns blazing and sort out body parts later."

"Yeah, about the guns and body parts bit, I guess maybe my movie experience isn't quite the boon I imagined it. I don't suppose you have an alternative?"

"Who, me?"

"Yes you."

"You want my help?"

She bit back a growl of annoyance as he teased her. Of all the bloody times to find his sense of humor, he had to choose now. "As a matter of fact, I do."

"Okay."

"And?"

"Oh, you want details?"

"Yes!"

He laughed. "Are you sure? You might be disappointed in it as it doesn't involve crashing into the asteroid or exploding it. Although, I do plan on making the environment unpleasant for any oxygen breathers."

"You mean the humans?"

"I mean the enemy." He said it so grimly that she decided not to point out he was technically human too, or at least began as one at birth. Despite his exterior, the ratio of man versus machine swung the pendulum, not necessarily in the right direction. Aphelion didn't look at her as he spoke, his eyes intent on his screen as his hands flew over his control panel. "I believe, if we punch a precise hole with our laser guns here and here." He pointed to an image, which he posted on the main viewing screen. "It will depressurize the whole installation and suck the oxygen out. It won't take care of all the soldiers, but those caught without masks or environmental suits will die, reducing the number of hostiles facing our troops. Not to mention, the remaining humans tend to panic when they start seeing corpses with bulging eyes and exploded brains floating about."

Her face scrunched up. "That is really gross."

"Just trying to live up to your cinematic expectation."

Snide little bugger. "You should know, Aphelion, I will get even."

"I look forward to it. Now, if you don't mind, we are entering firing range and I should probably concentrate on this next part. Please monitor the communications channels for any military activity, but before that, I'd like you to please send out a quick pulse followed by two long ones."

"Why?"

"Think of it as cyborg code for hold your breath and anchor your feet."

"Cool."

"Glad it meets your approval. Engaging laser systems."

As Aphelion steadied himself, she did as he asked, using the communications channel to broadcast the pulses. She just hoped Einstein and the others got it.

A voice crackled on the intercom. "Incoming vessels detected."

"From where?" she asked foolishly, peeking around.

"I don't see anything on the radar."

"Well then it must be broken," snapped the voice over the intercom, "because they are coming up fast on our tail."

"Who is that? And how come he can see ships when we can't?"

Aphelion frowned as his fingers flew lightning fast on his console. "That's Bolt down in engineering. He must be seeing the approaching spacecraft from our aft portholes. But why the hell aren't they showing up on our radar?"

"Don't worry about that now. Shoot the damn holes. Help the boys on the asteroid, then we can flip around and take care of the bogeys."

"Bogeys? I swear, if you begin to hum the theme from *Top Gun* like Seth did on our last mission, keep in mind I will shoot you myself," Aphelion muttered as his eyes narrowed.

Oddly enough, with all the technology at hand, he relied on an old style joystick to maneuver the exterior laser and fire. If the situation weren't so dire, she would have asked for a turn firing. She'd always enjoyed video games.

Watching the screen, she had time to note the quick light bursts, then a cloud of dust and gas as he scored dual hits on the asteroid surface. Two craters appeared, dust billowing outwards from them in rings. While she couldn't see the results, she could hear it. The installation depressurized and the communication channel came alive finally with the panicked yells of humans.

However, she didn't have time to listen because the first impact of a missile rocked their ship.

The bogeys had arrived and apparently, they weren't in the mood to take prisoners.

Chapter Twelve

The pulses broke through their radio silence. "Brace yourself," Einstein yelled, holding his fire and using his free hand to grip a rigid metal beam by the entrance to the loading bay. It seemed their ship caught wind of the ambush and came to the rescue.

"What the fuck? I told Aphelion to hang back," Aramus yelled, still aiming his weapon as he looped his arm around the post across from him.

"Who cares why he's here?" Seth shouted, his blades deflecting the shots whizzing their way from the soldiers who had them pinned at the corridor's entrance. "We could use a hand. There's too many of them for us to fight, and it's only a matter of time before one of them manages a lucky shot."

Einstein suspected Bonnie had a hand in the disobedience of Aramus' orders. While he hated she put herself in danger, he'd chide her for her disobedience later, once they escaped the military ambush. And ambush it was.

They soon discovered as they charged up the hall that the entire place was a fake. The doors they checked opened onto stone walls, except when they disgorged screaming soldiers. The first such wave took them by surprise and Aramus took a bullet to the leg before they adapted to the situation and fell into formation. In tight quarters, it proved difficult to use the guns with accuracy, making the need for knives and brute strength crucial, especially when they realized some of the soldiers were equipped with the latest Taser based weaponry. But Einstein had been slowly adapting the hardware in their bodies. He'd programmed the nanos, which coursed through their systems, to funnel electrical charges so that large bursts no longer incapacitated them. Of course, this was the first time they'd gotten a chance to test this new feature. To his scientific pleasure, his adaptations worked; the thousands of volts of energy aimed their way were unpleasant, but not debilitating.

Aramus grinned widely when a soldier aiming one of the enhanced Tasers muttered a disgusted, "Shit. It ain't workin' against the fucking bots."

Nope. It didn't. Not that the soldiers attacking cared for long. They dispatched that group. Then the one after, working their way along the trapped corridor toward the landing bay he'd detected on his scans.

They heard the signs of battle before reaching the open bay. It seemed their flanking brethren arrived before they did. Joining the firefight, they bunkered down by the opening and took turns firing on the horde of military grunts sitting behind reflective shields. The military came prepared for once, which meant it wasn't the easy assault Aramus expected.

Hence, the arrival of their ship and its subsequent warning to brace themselves, while unexpected, wasn't entirely unwelcome. It didn't clear out as many soldiers as Einstein would have liked, the troops hunkered behind their shields suited in protective space gear, but it took many of the humans by surprise. Environmental suits did little to help against the depressurization and suction of space, not to mention there were many who'd opted to remove their helmets. Dozens died. Unfortunately, dozens more remained to take their place. However, the humans were hampered by the new conditions, unlike the cyborgs. Their guns were of little use and their hand-to-hand combat and knife skills no match for the speed and strength of cyborgs. They sliced and diced their way through the remaining troops, not needing to worry about kill shots when even a simple slit in a space suit was enough.

Screams filled the air. Panic. Blood. Chaos reigned and at the heart of it all, the cyborgs fought, the two units meeting in the middle of the melee and placing themselves back to back, an impenetrable wall that fought back against the odds…and won.

Wiping the blood from his face—not his, but the enemies'—Einstein viewed the carnage and shook his head. "Why do they keep bothering? Why can't they just leave us alone?"

"And admit defeat?" Seth, not a hair out of place, sheathed his knives. "The military will never give up because they can't afford to have the world know what they did. How they lied. How they stole lives and experimented. The people would revolt if they suspected. Governments have after all toppled for less."

"But how can they explain this?" Einstein gestured around him. "What excuse can they give to the families of these soldiers?"

"Any damned one they please," Aramus replied. "They'll tell them the poor soldiers got attacked by hundreds of murdering robots. Robots intent on wiping out humanity. Not a bad idea actually, if you ask me."

"More killing isn't the answer."

"Then what is?" The question hung in air, heavily laden with the scent of death.

A shockwave rocked the asteroid, disturbing them from their intense discussion, one they'd had many a time over the years since they reached sentience.

"What the fuck?"

"I think our ship is in trouble," Seth announced.

Bonnie! Now that the need for subtlety was gone, Einstein reached out with his mind to their ship, but met with interference. "Dammit. I can't contact Aphelion or our vessel."

"We need to get back up there and see what's going on." But how? Their own craft lay at least an hour away even if they ran at full speed across the surface.

Why run though when they could ride? It was Seth who found the stashed buggies, each big enough to carry a pair of them. According to Astro, who met up with them on the battleground, Ralph and another comrade fell to the soldiers, both irreparably damaged after well-aimed shots to their cortexes. A grave loss to a cyborg nation who already numbered so few. However, regret would have to wait. Survival came first.

They sped across the asteroid surface to their hidden craft, Einstein straining to see overhead when he couldn't contact the ship despite his repeated attempts, but whatever happened in space remained out of sight and his worry mounted.

Please be safe.

Chapter Thirteen

Stupid movies, they make it look so easy and fun.

Bonnie kind of regretted taunting Aphelion to action. What she, in her inexperience and brashness, thought would be an easy task—rescue her lover and save the day—turned into a duel for their lives as not one or two, but three military cruisers popped out of nowhere and attacked. It was only the fact their hull survived the first hit and the skill of the skeleton crew in evading that kept them from splattering the asteroids they used as shields. It kind of reminded her of a large-sized game of keep away and chicken enacted in space where one wrong move would mean the end. Gulp.

Scary as it was, though, it wasn't the only problem.

When Luke Skywalker fought his cosmic battle with Darth Vader, swooping and spiraling through space, it made Bonnie whoop with excitement. In real life, all that motion just made her want to throw up. She'd never enjoyed roller coaster rides and becoming part machine hadn't changed that. Apparently, her programming and hardware didn't come with a cure for vertigo or motion sickness. Good thing she didn't eat and thus had nothing to spew; she doubted Aphelion would have appreciated wearing it. Not to mention,

149

she didn't want to disturb him, not with him doing his best to keep them alive.

Given his fast reflexes and his skill at maneuvering were all that kept them from a fiery death, she took back all her unkind thoughts on the serious cyborg. If he managed to keep them from getting blown into tiny bits, he deserved her heartfelt thanks and gratitude.

After a particularly stomach-churning flip, the vessel righted itself, thank God.

"That was close." His muttered words didn't inspire confidence, not that she could speak as he spun them again, a spiral loop that had her swallowing as she closed her eyes against the vertigo.

Aphelion, the surely insane cyborg, whooped. "Whee!"

"Ooooh," she moaned.

"What's wrong? I thought you liked action flicks. It doesn't get more action packed than this," he answered with all too much glee. And to think she'd accused him of being too serious.

"I like my action to remain upright, not upside down and spinning," she groaned.

He laughed. "And here I thought you had a more adventuresome spirit."

"And I can't believe I thought you had none."

"As Seth would say, suck it up, buttercup, it's not over yet."

A retort failed her so she resorted to something she hated—feminine whining. "Can't you just blow them up so we can stop hanging upside down like bats? My body was built for a lot of things, but screwing with gravity wasn't one of them."

"Wimp." He said it with mirth, but to her relief, the vessel straightened out and she slumped in her seat, glad he'd warned her to strap in. Although, she suspected his safety tip had less to do with her getting injured than his concern she'd smack into some important console by accident.

"Aha!"

She pried open one eye. "Is that a good aha?"

"We finally scored a hit on one of the ship's starboard engines. That makes another one out of commission. One to go."

Minutes later, the last military ship smacked into an asteroid as it miscalculated, probably because instead of firing on the enemy vessel, Aphelion shot up the big rock in front of them sending chunks of it spiraling off.

As soon as the military ship went up in a fiery explosion, the communication channel, which would only spew static since the ambush, began spewing messages from the cyborgs left behind on the asteroid.

"Aphelion!" Aramus bellowed, his irritable yell a welcome relief because it meant some of the cyborgs stuck amidst the ambush survived. "What the fuck is going on? And where the hell are you?"

But Bonnie only had ears for one voice and she fought not to choke up as she heard it.

"Bonnie, are you there? Answer me. Are you alright?"

She spoke aloud since Aphelion seemed to have engaged Aramus in the silent mode they could fall into. Lucky bastards with their wireless capabilities. She wouldn't have minded a little private time right about now with a certain geek she'd come to care entirely too much for.

Audience or not, she didn't bother to hide her happiness in hearing his voice. "I'm fine, charming. A little bit queasy from all the spinning, but unhurt. But what about you? Are you hurt? Did everyone make it? Did we arrive in time?"

"We're down two men. Ralph and Fred didn't survive the ambush. But the rest of us made it out with only a few holes and scratches. Nothing the nanos or I can't fix."

"Thank God."

"God had nothing to do with it. Skill and luck did. That and the disobedience of orders by a certain crew."

"Yeah, um, about that. Don't blame them. It was all my fault."

"I am sure it was. And don't worry, we'll be discussing that as soon as I get back onboard," Einstein said ominously.

Uh-oh. Sounded as if she was in trouble. Fine. Whatever. She wouldn't apologize for her actions. Much. Not when she'd probably repeat them. Einstein and the others had come to mean too much to her in the last few days since she'd woken for her to sit by idly while they were in danger. Hopefully, that would count for something. Besides, what was the worst they could do to her? *Spank me if I'm lucky.* Not that her geeky prince would think of that. Maybe she should suggest it.

However, seeing him face to face wouldn't happen as quickly as she liked. Looping back around, they rendezvoused with the scout ship. Unbuckling, she meant to scurry out to meet the returning cyborgs, but Aphelion shook his head. "Aramus says to sit your ass down and not move a muscle."

"Why, so he can punish me?"

"No, because he doesn't want Einstein distracted. As our only intelligence and medical officer, he needs to concentrate on fixing up our injured boys and getting this ship back in commission. We took some nasty hits and while most of us can do repair, we need his brain to reprogram some of our onboard controls to bypass the sections that were too badly damaged. Aramus doesn't want you diverting him from what needs to be done."

Well, that sucked. She'd wanted to see for herself that he was safe and sound. Give him a hug. A kiss. A… Hmmm. Maybe Aramus had a point. "Fine. I'll stay here out of sight and trouble."

"I wouldn't say out of trouble. The big boss is coming and he's pissed."

"At what? Us saving his ornery ass? He should be thanking us for coming to his rescue. Without us and those holes you blasted, they were toast."

"If you mean at a disadvantage, then probably, but at the same time, we broke the rules."

"You mean I did. Blame me if you like. I'll take any punishment he wants to dole out." Bonnie played the part of martyr well. Besides, what was the worst Aramus could do? Lock her up until they reached the cyborg home planet?

"You're not the only one at fault. I was also a part of it. I'll shoulder my share of the responsibility."

"Damned straight you will," Aramus roared as he stomped in. "What the fuck were you thinking of, letting a bloody female convince you to disobey orders?"

Aphelion stood and faced Aramus, covering her presence. As if the commander of the vessel didn't know she sat there. She did appreciate the gesture, though.

"She didn't force me to do anything. Once we realized the situation had radically changed, I analyzed the possible scenarios and came to the conclusion that without our aid, the landing party's chances of success were slim. Given our depleted numbers, as acting commander of the vessel, I did what I thought was best for the mission."

"And not only put the ship in danger, but one of the females too."

"This female has a name," she interjected.

"You, be quiet! I'll deal with you in a minute." Stormy eyes swung her way and she swallowed in reflex. Talk about scary-looking. Maybe she should worry for her safety.

"At the time, I didn't think our actions would put B785—"

She didn't think it was the time to point out her name was Bonnie.

"—in danger."

"No, you didn't think. Yet you should have. Your programming should have warned you of the possibility of enemy vessels lying in wait. As a result of your miscalculation, we almost lost the entire fucking ship and crew, not to mention one of the female cyborgs. What ended up a major cluster fuck almost turned into a disaster."

"You're right, sir. I was negligent in my duties and clearly unfit to serve. I will withdraw myself from active duty until I can submit myself for full diagnostic and repair."

"Denied. We need all the hands we can get." A heavy sigh left Aramus as with a heavy tread, he walked around a repentant—ass-kissing—Aphelion and headed for his seat, a seat she hastily vacated. Somehow, four hundred pounds of muscle and machine landing on her didn't seem healthy. "It's not entirely your fault, I guess. The way I hear it, the military ships didn't show up on any scans or our radars."

"No, sir, they didn't. None of our electronics detected them. It was pure chance they were spotted. We could only view them via the screening windows and exterior cameras, but that doesn't excuse my lapse. I should have obeyed orders and remained hidden. I accept any punishment you deem fit."

Bonnie jumped to his defense. "It's not his fault. I was the one who bugged him to do something."

Dark eyes swung her way. Aramus drummed his fingers on the armrest. "He knew better though than to disobey direct orders."

"Even if it saved your life?" she snapped.

"My life is meaningless if I don't bring you back intact. Do you have any idea of how important you've been deemed?" Aramus said it sourly. Apparently, he didn't agree. Oddly enough, Bonnie could understand him in that respect.

"Me, important? But why?"

"Joe is the leader of our movement. Chloe is his mate. Once they discovered we had recovered you alive, my one and only directive became to get you back safe."

"That's crazy. I'm not that important. Or special."

"On that we agree. But, it's not up to me. It's up to our society, and the cyborgs back home, your people and my brothers, have decided that rescuing you females takes top priority."

"But why?" Bonnie couldn't follow his logic. How could he and Einstein and the others be considered less important than her? *Don't they realize how flawed I am? How useless?* Other than her skill in the bedroom, what did she have to offer a planet full of men? Or was that why they valued her? Would her role on the cyborg planet end up similar to the one she served with the human military? She discarded the thought as soon as it hit. No. The cyborgs were different, and she believed Einstein when he said she'd have a choice in her future. Not to mention she couldn't believe the tender man who'd so reluctantly succumbed to her seduction thought of her as nothing more than a sexual object.

Someone else entered the command area, and she turned eagerly, hoping for a glimpse of Einstein, but instead, a disheveled Seth appeared. He flashed a grin. "Hey, princess. I hear you caused a mutiny then got in to a dogfight with the military? Way to go. Usually, I'm the only one capable of causing that much trouble. I thought Aramus would blow a gasket when he heard. You should have seen the smoke pouring from his ears."

"They disobeyed orders," Aramus growled.

"And saved our butts. Not to mention took out three bogeys. Bogeys that we couldn't detect and if left intact might have followed us back to the homeworld. If you ask me, their disobedience is the best thing that could have happened. Or would you have preferred being the reason why the military showed up on our doorstep?"

Poor Aramus. His face changed so many colors, she wondered for a moment if he'd have the first ever cyborg heart attack. "I'm leaving before I throttle you both. I'll be assessing the damage if anyone needs me." Off he stomped, easing the tension levels in the bridge.

Aphelion relaxed his rigid stance. "Well, that went better than expected."

"I'll say. Considering you have all your body parts intact and he didn't eject you into space, I'd say you lucked out, dude."

"For now. I doubt I've heard the last of it, though."

"Don't let him bully you," Bonnie advocated. "Aramus might talk tough, but at heart, I think he's more of a softy than he realizes." Two pairs of incredulous gazes swung her way. "What? Was it something I said?"

Shaking his head, Aphelion addressed Seth. "Sir, if I may. Einstein has requested an extra pair of hands for aid in repairing our cloaking device. I'd like leave to go help him."

He had? Damned silent talk. She really hated she wasn't a part of those conversations. The fun she could have silently conversing with her prince charming. Then again, the kind of talk she'd enjoy was best done in person where she could see her prince's blushing reaction.

"Go, soldier. But you'll need to submit a full report of the events as soon as you're done. Even if Aramus skipped punishment, we still need to let Joe and the others know what happened here as soon as possible."

"Yes, sir. Oh and just so you know, only two of the three attacking ships were destroyed. The third vessel crash landed on an asteroid."

"Intact?"

"To a certain extent."

"You can see them now?"

"Yes. Whatever technology made them invisible didn't survive the impact so I've had our computers monitoring it. According to what we could see and detect, the damage was extensive. Life support systems appear to have failed, making survivors unlikely."

"But possible if they got into a pod or a space suit." Seth rubbed his chin. "What about their communications?"

"Inactive as far as we can tell. Unless they sent out a signal beforehand or are using some new method of transmission, they haven't contacted anyone."

"However, there's no way of knowing for sure, just like we can't be sure there's no other enemy vessels lurking in the area." Seth paced.

"No, sir."

"Fuck." Seth bore the most serious expression she'd ever seen. It frightened Bonnie because it seemed so out of place on his usually jovial face. "Go help Einstein and tell Aramus what you told me. We need to make a quick decision on what to do."

"You mean leave before military reinforcements arrive?" she said, drawing his attention.

"Bingo, princess. Our prime directive, despite this setback, is still to get you to safety."

"Are we back to that again?" She rolled her eyes. "You all realize I am just one person. One severely messed up, not all that important girl. Just ask Aramus."

"His opinion doesn't count. He says that about pretty much everyone. And don't downplay yourself. You might not put much credence in your worth, but according to Chloe, Joe, and a planet full of cyborgs, you're irreplaceable. I think you're pretty neat, myself, and I'm fairly certain Einstein would rate you as priceless."

The idea Einstein valued her so highly both elated and deflated her. She didn't deserve that kind of adoration—even if she yearned for it. "I say you're all nuts. You can't mean to tell me you're just going to fly away from a military vessel without getting some answers."

"We should. Getting out of the area before more military troops arrive makes the most sense."

"But if it weren't for me, you wouldn't. You'd be boarding that downed spacecraft, grabbing everything you could, like hard drives and stuff, and most of all, trying to figure out how the hell they snuck up on us."

"Maybe." Seth wouldn't meet her gaze as he studied the information on the screen he perused.

"Don't you maybe me. The military almost caught us."

"They did."

"They managed to bypass all the detection systems."

"Yup."

"Oh come on. Even my little girly cyborg brain knows that's bad. More than bad, it's seriously dangerous, and important, a lot more important than me. Much as my sister loves me, and your planet supposedly needs me as some kind of rallying poster girl, you need to find out how the military did it. We need the technology on that ship."

"We do."

"And don't even think of arguing. Wait. Did you just say we do?"

Facing her finally, Seth let out a weary sigh. "Yeah. I did. Despite what Joe and the others want, you are right. We can't allow this opportunity to go to waste. We need to get our hands on whatever device or programming the military has created that's allowing them to hide themselves from our detection systems. It was one thing for them to have bugs we couldn't locate. But ships? That puts our whole world at risk."

Lifting her hands and eyes to the ceiling she sang, "Hallelujah! Finally, someone sees the light."

"Yup, but now it's going to be convincing a certain someone that risking you to search the ship while keeping an eye out for bogeys is important enough to ignore direct orders."

"If you mean Aramus, I'll take care of him."

"I'd pay to watch that. But, no, he'll actually see the sense in staying. The person I'm talking about is Einstein."

Oh please, as if her gentle prince charming wouldn't see the logic. How wrong she was.

Chapter Fourteen

Despite the urge to see how Bonnie fared—and hug her close, which made no sense as it wasn't a proper diagnostic method for establishing injury—Einstein worked tirelessly to repair both his comrades and the ship. With the exception of some missing fingers on Astro's hand from a gun blast, he was able to resolve most of the medical issues while the nanobots in their bodies took care of the rest. Brethren patched up, he then moved on to helping out with the more crucial items crippling their ship. Some rooms in the stern required sealing off until they could perform a spacewalk or land somewhere stable and weld the holes left by the blasts. A bit of rerouting on the subroutines bypassed some of the non-needed functions minimizing the damage to certain electrical components.

All in all, things could have been much worse. The majority survived. Bonnie was unhurt—apparently. He'd yet to verify for himself and probably wouldn't relax until he did. As soon as the engines powered up and they could get on their way, he intended to hunt her down and check her status—then kiss her, among other things. Despite not knowing how she fit in his regimented life, and what she expected from him, of one thing he was certain—he wanted more of what she had to give.

Tasks completed, or at least the ones requiring his physical hands, he went looking for the female who occupied his thoughts. He found her on the observation deck, staring out into space, the viewing window having survived the space battle due to Aphelion smartly lowering the metal blind to block off any direct damage.

Seeing her standing there, so pensive, her expression in profile sad, made his eager step slow. Then stop. The entire time he'd fought and then worked, she'd hovered at the edges of his mind, his need to perform his duty warring with a strong one that demanded he find her and protect her. Hold her. Keep her safe.

Since the moment they'd shared coitus, more than ever, he found himself conflicted where she was concerned. How did she feel about him? What did he feel for her? Why did he feel? Why did his mind whirl when she was around? His heart, body, and logic malfunctioned when she drew near. He wished he understood this disturbing phenomenon, or could find the answers. But clarity eluded him and having always been the smartest cyborg around, he didn't know who to turn to for aid.

And now, with Bonnie staring away from him, knowing he stood there, not acknowledging him, he wondered if he should stay or go. Did she want to be alone? Was he unwelcome? Did...

"Oh God, Einstein. I was so scared," she whispered in the silence, her arms wrapping around her upper torso.

The soft admission hit him and all of his hardware froze for a moment. He didn't know what to reply. Guilt assailed him at her admittance. He'd failed her. They all had. Logic insisted the blame wasn't his—even if a part of him believed it was. Not that he admitted that aloud. "The fight could have been avoided if you'd obeyed Aramus' orders to stay out of sight."

"Not scared for me, charming," she uttered with exasperation as she whirled to fix him with her jeweled gaze. "Scared for you. You could have died down there."

She'd worried for him? "I didn't die, though. I barely got scratched." To his surprise. His lessons with Seth paid off.

"Ralph and Fred weren't so lucky," she pointed out.

"No. They weren't, and the way I hear it, it was pretty close there for awhile for you and the ship's crew as well."

She shrugged. "I guess. At the time, though, I wasn't thinking about dying, although I did scream inside my head a lot. Aphelion really knows how to fly this thing. I just wish it didn't involve so much spinning. I almost barfed on him a few times." She rubbed her tummy with a rueful smile.

He latched on to the one thing he understood. "I can help you with the vertigo when we get to my lab. I'm pretty sure we've got a program for that, which I can download to your BCI."

"Really?" Her expression brightened. "I'd like that. But you're changing the subject."

"You're right, I am, because otherwise I might be tempted to launch in to a discourse about how Aphelion's actions put you in unacceptable danger. Actually, the entire decision to explore the asteroid was ill advised. We should have known better than to jeopardize your safety. That won't happen again. From this point on, our only objective is to get you home where you'll be safe."

"Einstein, we can't go to your world yet."

"Oh yes we can. As soon as we can be sure no one's on our tail, we are heading to the base."

"But that's just it, will it be safe? I was talking to Seth—"

"Oh no. No good ever comes of a conversation with him."

"Let me finish. I was talking to Seth and he agrees that we can't leave without checking out that crashed ship."

As if Einstein cared what Seth or anyone else thought. "Yes, we can. And we will. We've already placed you in enough danger. I've already sent out a request to have a clean vessel meet us in a few days time to transfer you."

"Transfer me?"

"Since we can't be sure this ship is clean, and given our current damage, we need to get you—"

Hands planted on her hips, she fixed him with a fierce glare. "You need to get me nowhere. I am perfectly fine where I am. You're being illogical."

"I am never illogical."

"Oh yes you are, because if it weren't for me, you'd be the first one to advocate finding out what technology is currently hidden on that downed military craft. What secrets might lie within the hard drives. What they knew about our plans."

In normal circumstances, yes, he would, but things were anything but normal. "It can wait."

"No it can't, and you know it. Why are you being so irrational?"

"It's not irrational to obey orders."

"It is, especially when those orders didn't take into account what we'd encounter. There is an opportunity here for us to discover what the military is up to. That is way more important than me. I'm just one person. A flawed female cyborg. A nobody. Meanwhile, that ship has some programming or technology that might save hundreds of cyborgs. Or give us answers."

How could she think so lowly of herself? Did she not understand her importance? Her worth? "We'll get our answers, just not at your expense."

"How is delaying our departure for a salvage mission putting me in danger?"

"We need to leave the area in case more troops arrive."

"We need to board that ship."

"It can wait."

"No, it can't!" She yelled. "Stop being so stubborn. You keep saying this is all about me, well, don't I get a say? Didn't you tell me that part of being a cyborg was having a choice? A say in my fate? Well, my vote is we grab as much shit off that military vessel as we can and then run."

"No."

"Yes."

"No."

"Why are you being so pigheaded?"

A part of Einstein realized she made good points, and yes, she should have say in matters pertaining to her, yet something other than logic drove him at this point. Hot, angry, and not in charge of the words spewing from his mouth, he shouted, "I don't care if it's irrational or the right thing. We are not staying here. Or exploring that ship. Not happening. I can't go through that again. You don't understand what it was like during the battle. And then after, knowing the ship fought against wretched odds."

Her eyes widened at his outburst, but she didn't shy from his anger. "You were scared?"

Funny how she could so easily pinpoint what bothered him. Not having truly experienced fear before, he'd not recognized it. Yet another new defect. "Yes, I feared."

"It's normal. Battles are scary."

Now who was acting dense? He shook his head. "Not scared for me, Bonnie. Like you, I feared for your life."

167

"But why? Is it because of your orders to deliver me safely?"

"Partially."

"Because we had sex?"

"Yes. No. Maybe."

"Care to add any more answers?" A teasing smile tilted her lips.

And suddenly, a torrent came rushing out of him and he bared his innermost confusing thoughts to her. "Don't you get it? You're important to me. I don't understand why or how it happened; despite all the arguments, your safety is of paramount importance to me. I can't help it. When the ambush hit, all I could think of was thank fuck you were on the ship, and out of danger's way. But then you arrived to my rescue, put yourself in harm's way, and when I realized that, I thought the hardware powering my organs would fail. I couldn't think. Couldn't function. I—I—feared. Feared I'd lose you. I won't allow myself to go through that awful sensation again."

Closing the gap between them, she almost ran and he opened his arms, pulling her tight to him in a hug. She felt so frail in his embrace. So small. Once again, he realized how close he came to losing her and his throat tightened. He closed his eyes as he leaned his chin against the top of her head. For a long silent moment, they stood thus entwined. Her fingers toyed with the tips of his hair. "It wasn't a malfunction, Einstein. It's called emotions. You care for me. That's why you were scared. That's why you're not able to think rationally. You feel affection for me and want to keep me safe. It's normal. It's part of being human."

"I'm not human. I'm a cyborg. A robot. Unlike the others, I changed too much. I don't feel."

"Yes, you do." She peered up at him and cupped his cheeks, forcing him to look at her. "Part machine or not, you just thought yourself incapable of emotion. And yet, you experience it every day. I've seen it. Would a machine with no sentiment engage his comrades like you do? I've seen you converse with Seth and the others. Joke. Laugh and talk. Would a robot with no fervor react as you do? Would a being with no heart burn with such passion? Treat me with such gentleness? Care for me as if I were the most precious of things?"

"But you are precious."

"To you." She smiled, a soft smile to go along with the fingers gently brushing his skin. "If you were truly only a robot relying only on logic, then you would see that the safety of one does not trump that of hundreds. But, your humanity is refusing to let you succumb to common sense. Your heart is telling your machine side to shut the fuck up and do what you feel is right. You, my dear and oblivious prince charming, are not defective. You quite simply care."

Care? Could he really? It seemed like such a small word to explain everything he felt. Perhaps because it was the wrong word. He summarized some of his chaotic thoughts into a more organized fashion, examining them in light of her allegation. He felt responsible for her. Protective. Jealous. Attracted. Possessive.

A new, even scarier conclusion arose as the proper definition for his emotions emerged.

I love her. What else could explain it? All the emotions he'd imagined himself incapable of, the things he'd attributed to malfunctions, they all had an explanation. He loved Bonnie. Amazing and irrational as it seemed, despite all the modifications done to him, he still had the capacity to love. It stunned him. "You're right. I do care. Very much."

"I don't know why you sound so surprised."

"Emotions are hormonal imbalances. I control my hormonal levels. Or did until I met you."

She wrinkled her nose and laughed. "You know that wasn't exactly the most romantic declaration."

"I didn't realize my words were meant to be a romantic declaration. I was just stating my current state of mind."

"Let me clear it up for you. I think I've fallen in love with you, Einstein."

She loved him too? No. He couldn't be so lucky. Bonnie was too good for him. Too beautiful and perfect. Too everything. "You're just appreciative of the fact I found and rescued you from certain destruction."

"No. Unlike you, I know what I'm feeling. It's love. L.O.V.E. Look it up because this is going to sound presumptuous of me, but since you have a problem with the obvious, I'm pretty sure you love me too."

He did, but his tongue couldn't push the word past his lips. What did he have to offer her? He was a science geek among his brethren. The weakest in battle. The smallest cyborg among a horde of giants. She deserved so much better.

"I can see you're still not sure. Let me ask you, does what I've told you about my past bother you?"

"No. Of course not." How could she think that?

"What about the thought of me with another man?"

He growled, a primitive sound he would have never thought himself capable of making.

"When we reach your homeworld, what would you do if I walked away and started a new life without you?"

Pressure crushed the mechanical organ pumping enhanced blood to his extremities. His mind wavered between rage and anguish. He couldn't help whispering, "You can't. I need you." Even if she deserved someone more capable of keeping her safe.

She hugged him. "Oh, Einstein. I'm sorry. I didn't mean I would, I was just using it as an example. You love me. What more proof do you need, charming? There is no proven test for love. You just know it. Live it."

"I do know it. But…"

"But what?"

"You deserve better. Someone bigger and stronger. Someone who can fight and protect you from danger."

"You fought."

"Not nearly half as well as the others," he admitted to his shame.

"Did it ever occur to you that I don't want a thug who knows how to use his fists or knives? That perhaps I like a man who's smart?"

"You say that now, but you've yet to meet the others on the planet. There are cyborg units with some modicum of intelligence and skills. Cyborgs better than me."

"Oh, charming. Don't you get it? Love doesn't work that way. I don't love you because you can protect me, or because of how you look. I love you because you're you. Would you stop loving me if you met a prettier cyborg girl with a nicer past?"

He met her gaze, angry that she'd even suggest such a thing. His indignant tone relayed some of it when he replied. "Of course not."

"Then why would you think me so shallow? Despite the fact I don't understand why you love me, I would never leave you. I couldn't, Einstein. You're my prince charming. The one person in this whole universe capable of reaching the heart and soul I thought I'd lost. The one man who can make me feel. The only man I've ever truly loved so much that I would rather die than see you come to harm."

"Then why won't you let me take you away from here? If you love me so much and if this is what I feel, why can't I put you somewhere safe?"

"Because we're cyborgs. And cyborgs do what's right for their kind, even if that means putting the needs of others ahead of our own."

Courage and moral conviction. Was it possible to love her even more? He borrowed an expression from Seth. "That sucks."

"Don't pout. It's way too cute, and we have things to do before I can suck on that delectable lower lip of yours."

"Do we have to?"

"We should."

He sighed. "I'd still prefer to put you somewhere safe."

"I know, charming. But it will have to wait. We need what's hiding on that ship. While I might be smarter than you when it comes to affairs of the heart, you're still the smartest geek around. You want to keep me safe, then look at this way—you need to put that genius of yours to work and find out what those military jerks are up to, because then and only then can you truly protect me. "

Put that way, she made a valid point. "Fine. You win. We'll salvage what we can from the military vessel, but only if you promise to stick by my side, here on the ship where it's safe."

"Deal."

"Really?"

"Well duh. Even I know I don't look good in a space suit."

"You always look good to me."

"Mmm," she purred. "Remember to say that to me again when we're alone in your room."

"Why?"

"You'll like the result." She nibbled his lower lip and he groaned because now he could too clearly imagine the result. And damn, he could already hypothesize it would be explosive.

Why wait? When she would have broken off their kiss, he caught her face between his hands and continued the embrace.

"What." Mmm. "Are." Lick. "You doing?" she mumbled against his mouth.

"Things can wait a few minutes."

"They can?"

"Oh yes," he purred, a sound a few weeks ago he'd never imagined himself capable of making. "I've got something more important to take care of first."

"You do?"

"Definitely. Think of it as your punishment for scaring the hell out of me." He nipped her lip before sucking on her tongue.

"Mmm. You know this isn't punishment."

Zipper opened, he slid his hand inside her jumpsuit and he found her already wet. Wet, hot, and oh so ready for him. He dipped a finger into her channel and she gasped. He murmured, "I'm not done yet."

With a slowness that made her clench, he finger fucked her, swallowing her gasps, teasing her until she shuddered against him. How he would have liked to prolong this moment forever, but even he knew the clock ticked. Down he tugged the rest of her jumpsuit until it pooled around her feet.

A part of him understood they didn't really have time for this, that someone could come looking at any moment. Hell, he'd already mentally projected a couple of "Fuck offs!" to Aramus and the others when they tried to mindspeak to him. He needed this moment with Bonnie. Needed it before they faced the unknown and danger again.

Lifting her, he pressed her back against the window, the stars a twinkling backdrop, the sharp contrast of black space making her skin seem even more luminous and perfect. Her legs wrapped around his waist, aligning her with the tip of him. He held off for a moment, though, rubbing his swollen head against her wet slit, loving how she gasped, watching how her eyes shut and her head tilted back, her passion for him so clear. He wanted to freeze time. Keep them in this moment forever. But he was cyborg. Duty awaited, a duty she understood and encouraged.

"I love you," he uttered in a low tone.

Lashes fluttered as she opened her eyes, her green jeweled gaze capturing his. "I love you too, charming. Now stop being such a tease and fuck me."

Yeah, that was his Bonnie. To the point, not as delicate as she seemed, and his. *All mine.*

One thrust and he sheathed himself within her. She cried out. "Yes!"

Oh yes. Warm, wet, and wild, her body drew him in, her inner muscles squeezing as he pumped her, drawing out each stroke, maximizing the moment. But she didn't want it slow.

"Fuck me," she growled. "Fuck me, charming. Fuck me like only you can."

The dirty words, which from anyone else would have perturbed him, enflamed him because they were for him. It was he who drove her nuts with passion. His body, his cock she wanted. And he gave it to her, thrusting, hard and fast, in and out until her fingers dug into his shoulders, and her mouth rounded into a silent scream.

He wasn't so quiet. He yelled her name as he came, his hot spurt triggering her own orgasm, the muscles of her sex squeezing and undulating along his length.

In that moment, he wasn't a cyborg. Or a human. He was simply alive. Alive and in love. It felt fucking great.

Chapter Fifteen

Breathless and sated in his arms, Bonnie couldn't bring herself to regret admitting her love for him. Selfish or not, she couldn't deny herself the happiness, not when he admitted how he felt. What purpose would hurting them both serve? So what if he was too good for her? She had the rest of her life to prove she deserved him. The rest of her life to atone for her past. The rest of her life to love him.

Slowly, he let her go, his reluctance clear. She understood it only too well. They'd both just taken a huge leap in their relationship. This was a moment they would remember and cherish forever. It deserved a certain solemnity. However, duty called. People waited on them.

"We really should get back to the others."

For a moment, he didn't reply. His hands wandered her body and against her lower belly, his cock, still semi-hard, pressed slickly.

"They can wait a little longer."

"They'll come looking if we don't get back to them with an answer."

"Screw them."

"Charming!" God, she was such a bad influence on him.

"What? We're about to head into possible danger. Who knows when we'll have a moment like this again? I've done my duty for years. If I want to take a few minutes and be selfish, then damn it all, I will."

"You know Aramus will blame me."

"He better not or I'll have him singing show tunes," Einstein growled.

She giggled. "That's just mean."

"For everyone who has to listen."

The devilish grin on his face had her laughing. "Oh and to think I used to think you lacked a sense of humor."

"I did until I met you. I might have woken you from your sleep, but you woke me to my humanity."

If she could have shed tears, she would have; as it was, her throat tightened. "Now that was romantic."

"It was?"

"Most definitely." She kissed him. She only meant to do so softly in thank you, but he had other ideas. Hungry as if they'd not just assuaged their passion, he devoured her mouth, his tongue seeking hers for a hot duel that roused the heat that always seemed to simmer when he was around.

"We really should get going."

"We will. When I'm good and ready," he murmured back. "I have a problem that needs tending first."

"Is it hard?"

"Oh yes."

"Distracting?"

"Very much so. Enough that I could never concentrate on the task at hand."

Turning in his grasp, she tossed him a coy smile over her shoulder. "We can't have that now, can we?"

"Nope." Over she bent, waggling her bottom at him. He stepped up behind her and with his cock gripped in one hand, rubbed himself against her. She moaned.

"We need to make this quick," she gasped.

"I don't think that will be a problem." Grasping one of her shoulders, he pushed into her and she moaned. Her already sensitized pussy quivered around him, their new position according him a new angle to penetrate her. Deeply he thrust, the head of his dick hitting her sweet spot, but as if that weren't enough, his fingers also found her clit and rubbed.

"Yes, yes, yes," she chanted as they rocked in unison.

"Hey Einstein, how come you're not answering…" Seth's intruding voice trailed off. "Um, I see you're busy, but, uh, well, you know we're kind of all waiting on you."

"Get out," Einstein grunted, not slowing his pace.

"Is this going to take long?"

Bonnie almost screamed it wouldn't if he'd leave. Thankfully, Einstein spoke for both of them. "Get out before I program you to wear dresses and makeup and rename you Sally," he yelled.

"Testy. Testy. When you're done, mind meeting us in the control room? We have decisions to make."

"Fuck off!"

Bonnie wisely didn't giggle as Seth purposely drove her lover insane. Their fault for choosing such a public place. What amazed her more than their location was the fact Einstein didn't withdraw or retreat into his usual shy shell at the interruption. Nope. The sexual monster she'd created didn't lose his erection or his pace, although he did shift in such a way as to hide her from his friend's view. And women thought chivalry was dead.

"I'm leaving. Geez. You know sex is supposed to relax you, right? Oh and just so you know, that window isn't polarized."

Which meant anyone outside the ship could be watching? Unlikely, given their location in space, but somehow exciting. Einstein must have thought so too because he pounded her furiously as soon as they heard the distinctive snick of the door sliding shut. Flattening her palms against the glass, she took it, and begged for more. Begged him to fuck her. To claim her. To love her.

Despite what would happen in the next few hours, they'd at least found a few things, other than nirvana. A chance for a future. Hope. And best of all, love. A love Bonnie would do everything in her power to hold on to. *The military is not taking this away from me.* Not without a fight.

Chapter Sixteen

Sated, quickly cleaned up and dressed again, they finally made it to the meeting and walked into a roomful of smirks and one gigantic scowl.

"About time you fucking showed up," Aramus snarled.

Considering where he'd prefer to be—between Bonnie's thighs where everything in the universe seemed perfect—Einstein calmly flipped his middle finger, which sent Seth into hysterics, saw Aphelion hiding his face behind his hand, and Aramus steaming. "Bonnie and I had things to discuss."

"Wish I could have more discussions of that sort," Seth whispered to Nova.

The old Einstein would have blushed, but the new one? He took a seat beside his lover and grinned. "You can all be jealous of me later. What have we discovered about the downed ship? According to the reports I gleaned on the way over, no hostiles have been reported. The communications channels are silent and there are no signs of activity that we can perceive. Correct?"

Seth gaped at him. "Dude, when did you have time to ascertain all that?"

"Some of us know how to multitask."

"I can vouch for his skill in that area," Bonnie added, her innuendo finally bringing heat to his cheeks.

Clearing his throat, Einstein veered the topic back in the right direction. "After analyzing the situation, running some hypothetical scenarios and statistical probabilities, I see no reason why we shouldn't investigate the crash site and see what we can salvage."

"Our orders from Joe are to bring Bonnie to the rendezvous point as soon as possible," Aramus replied as he drummed his thick fingers on the table in hard staccato bursts. "Once she's on her way, then we're clear to return and check the ruins out."

"Waiting might mean we lose our chance at discovering what the military is doing, though. I think we should grab what we can now. We are here, after all." Serious for once, Seth made his position clear.

"Agreed. My statistics say the likelihood of anything salvageable remaining if we delay at less than eight percent. This is our window of opportunity," Einstein added.

"We have orders."

Bonnie sat up straight in her seat. "Orders pertaining to me, which means I should get a say. And as I told my prince charming here, I say that getting all the intel we can is more important than getting my ass out of here. When else will we get a chance like this?"

"Are you asking me to counteract a direct command?" Aramus met her gaze with a dark one of his own.

"I think the situation warrants it," Einstein said, adding his voice to her argument. "Joe is our leader, I don't dispute that, but in this instance, he's speaking with his heart, not logic. An hour ago, I would have agreed with him. Bonnie is important. Really important. But, she's right when she says we might not get another opportunity like this. These military ships have some kind of new technology, something that renders them invisible on our radars. We need to find out what it is. Our whole world is in danger if we don't."

Bonnie, a serious look on her face, met Aramus' gaze and held it, not a feat many could manage when he wore his vicious scowl. "I'd like to also add that my life won't be worth squat if the military can track and follow us without us being the wiser. I'd say that trumps everything at this point. I know Joe means well and he's acting on behalf of my sister. Trust me, the importance you are all placing on me is flattering beyond belief, but I am just one cyborg. The needs of all must come before one."

"For a PITA, you're making sense for once," Aramus answered, in less of a grumpy tone than usual.

"Aah, a compliment. Quick, someone mark it on a calendar."

"I take it back."

"Too late. We all heard it. You're no longer the heartless Tin Man from Oz. Next thing we know, you'll be singing show tunes."

"Einstein, muzzle her before I throttle her."

"Touch her and you'll be singing soprano." Einstein said it with a deadpan expression that made Aramus' brows rise. "Besides, you won't have to listen much longer because since we're all in agreement, we should get moving. Who knows how long we've got before someone comes to investigate. We need to get a small team in and out as soon as possible."

"Any idea what we're looking for?"

I wish. The not knowing was what bothered him most. Einstein shrugged. "Nope. This new technology has me stumped. I never did figure out what those new bugs we pulled from previous missions were made of, so chances are, whatever we're looking for won't show up with our usual scanners, which means you'll need to rely on your visual senses."

"In other words, whatever doesn't come up on the screen but we can see with our eyes is what we want to take."

"Exactly."

"Gotcha, dude. I volunteer to be part of the boarding crew." Seth raised his hand and in minutes, they'd decided who would go and who would remain behind. Only the most observant were chosen to go: Seth, Nova, Astro, and Bolt would scour the downed military vessel.

Aramus didn't seem happy at the decision to have him remain behind, but as Seth pointed out, of them all, his eyesight was the worst. "I'll oversee the operation with Einstein in the command center. The rest of the crew will man portholes on all sides of our ship to watch for incoming. Aphelion, I'll want you sitting on the lasers, ready to defend us. PITA, you'll be on the com system. You hear anything and you let me fucking know. While retrieving data and hardware is important, we still don't want to be taking any stupid chances. Any questions?" Heads swiveled all around, but no one had anything to add. "Then let's get moving. I don't want to be hanging around here too long in case the military decides to show up with a fucking armada. Good luck, everyone."

"And may the force be with you," Bonnie added, to which Seth began to hum a tune that Bonnie and a few others joined in, something Einstein's memory banks called the "Imperial March." Apparently, the catchy song referenced a seventies cult movie series titled *Star Wars*. Trust his lover to turn a serious situation into something light, but it eased the tension in the room.

As for the images he filtered of a certain princess from said movie in skimpy attire? It certainly gave him ideas for later when he got Bonnie to safety.

Chapter Seventeen

Stupid overprotective cyborg males.

Once again, Bonnie was left behind to watch as others went off on an adventure, but this time, she at least had Einstein at her side because as Aramus stated, "I need someone to keep PITA in line."

Ha, as if her prince charming could stop her from acting if she chose. Actually, he was the one person who probably could—if he asked nicely.

Using the same shuttle they'd used to visit the asteroid, the chosen four left quickly once the decision to investigate was made. It didn't take them long to land and make their way to the vessel, a beached metal whale on an alien moon, or so her imagination compared it. Via cameras mounted to the helmets of those chosen to go, she and the others watched as the cyborg boarding party entered through a hull breach on the downed ship. Having watched many an alien movie during her teenage years, Bonnie bit her lip, visions of attacking aliens shooting electrical sparks and zombielike human crewman lurking in the darkness vivid in her mind. The reality was much more boring. The downed craft showed not a sign of life. A layer of silt already covered the interior, the insides basically space junk—torn metal, hanging wires, and bodies caught in the wreckage. Despite the fact they'd tried to kill her, she still winced at the sight. Death was always ugly.

A whistle came from Seth. "What a mess. I don't know if we'll be able to find anything useful in this."

"You're currently seeing the worst of the damage," Einstein noted via communicator to the landing party. "That's where the missile impacted and sliced through their hull. It's also the side that hit the asteroid first. Lucky for us, this area of the ship belonged to crew's quarters and storage."

Lucky for them perhaps, not to so much for the crew. Although, most of them were probably at their work stations doing their best to kill the cyborg menace, Bonnie did her best to squash her sympathy. The humans would have had none for her.

Einstein continued. "The engines themselves, which are a level down, while impacted during the crash, should be more or less intact. Nova and Bolt, head to your left and see if you can get to the engine room. What we want is probably attached to their main power reactor. Or so I assume. Logic says any technology that could hide a vessel of that size would require lots of energy to power it. So it should be around there somewhere. The problem with assumptions, though, is I don't want us to blind ourselves to what they really should be looking for. It could be anything. Or anywhere."

"Too late to worry about that now," Bonnie said softly. "Relying on common sense is all we have for the moment."

"What about us?" asked Astro. "Where do you want us to go?"

"Seth and Astro, you guys—"

"Will go the other way," Seth interrupted. "I know, dude. Just chill and watch for weird shit. We know what we're doing."

And they probably did, under normal circumstances. Problem was, Einstein and the others didn't know what they were looking for. Big machine. Little one. Her poor geek. Bonnie could see a part of him wished he'd fought harder to go with the group.

Splitting his attention between the search parties, her lover tried to give them equal attention as they delved deeper, wending their way through dark halls. Bonnie had to wonder at their decision to send so few. Then again, if the military unexpectedly showed up, more hands on deck meant a greater chance they could prevail and rescue the small party on the ground.

Despite what Hollywood led her to expect, no slavering green Martians with big teeth and an appetite for human flesh jumped out at any of them. A good thing, and yet at the same time, kind of disappointing.

Not long into their journey, Bolt and Nova encountered a shut door in their path, one which refused to budge no matter how they strained, the metal bent from impact. Since they had to stop and pull out a blowtorch to try and cut their way through, Einstein switched most of his attention to Seth and Astro.

The pair encountered no obstacles they couldn't clamber around in their trek; however, at a split in the corridor, they needed to make a decision. "Dude, which way should we go first? According to schematics, left is the captain's quarters, while right is the command center."

"Captain's rooms."

"Command center."

Einstein and Aramus both spoke at the same time. Aramus thumped his fist on his armrest. "I'm fucking in charge of this mission and I say they go to the command area."

Meeting his glare, Einstein's lip thinned as he stood up to him. "I'm ship's intelligence officer and strategist. I say they go to the captain's rooms for logs and communication."

In an attempt to lighten the tense mood, Bonnie bounced up from her seat, placing herself between them and breaking their staring match. "Yay. I get to be the tie breaker."

"Stay out of this, PITA."

"Her name is Bonnie."

"Whatever. It's not her call. I say we arm wrestle for it," Aramus growled.

"Ha. Like I'll fall for that. I've got a better idea. Why don't we solve an equation?" Einstein countered.

"Why don't you just have them split up?" Bonnie suggested, unable to keep quiet.

"Already done, princess," Seth said over the intercom. "I'm heading to the captain's quarters while Astro heads to the main controls."

Clapping her hands, she beamed. "Solution found."

Einstein almost laughed at Aramus' sour look. "So it seems. Aramus, why don't you keep an eye on Astro while I watch Seth?" At his grunt of assent, Einstein tuned into his screen and Bonnie, earpiece firmly attached, listened for any sign of hostiles as she leaned over his shoulder to take a peek.

"This place is spooky," Seth muttered.

"Are you worried about the captain's ghost popping out?" Bonnie teased.

"Hey, don't laugh. Last time the boys and I thought we might have run into a ghost, we ended up finding F814."

"Seriously?"

"Yup. She was haunting the mines on this asteroid we were checking out. So don't laugh. Who knows what could pop out?"

"You don't think they had any cyborgs aboard, do you?" Einstein asked.

Seth shrugged, or so she assumed given the jiggle of the camera. "You never know. The soldiers we encountered on the asteroid said something about reprogramming us. Who knows what the military has been doing. Maybe we'll find out. I'm here." Stopping before a door identical to the others except for the military fleet emblem, Seth yanked off the control panel. Without power, the usual mechanics didn't respond to touch. He yanked on the manual lever, releasing the latch. A click sounded. Slipping his fingers into a groove along the edge, Seth slid the door open and stepped in.

Chaos reigned, but less because of the crash and more because the captain was a slob. Clothes lay strewn about, along with dirty dishes and other detritus.

"What a pig," Seth exclaimed.

"Perhaps he was too busy to clean up," Einstein said.

"Too busy to throw it down a chute for someone else to clean? Whatever, dude. Where should I begin looking? I warn you, though, I ain't going anywhere near his underwear drawer without gloves."

Bonnie stifled a giggle.

"See if you can locate his desk. There should be a console built into it. Even with the power out, it should be a simple matter to pop the hard drive with the files I'm looking for."

"On it. Anything else?"

"Put your camera on rotation while you get it and I'll tell you what else to grab if I see anything."

"What are you looking for?" Bonnie asked.

"A lot of military captains keep a separate journal, usually a paper notebook or an electronic storage device not connected to the mainframe. A safety net just in case something bad happens and the military wipes certain missives in an attempt to screw them over."

"How sad. Even their own soldiers don't trust them."

"Would you?"

Of course not, but she had valid reason. Then again, having seen how the military acted during her tenure with them, was it any surprise their own officers would want backup in case shit hit the fan? She watched intently with Einstein as the camera panned the room. Clothes, boots, magazines with naked boobies, more clothes, dirty dishes, a few picture frames, which Einstein zoomed in on. They depicted a rather boring-looking man in a uniform with an older couple. The same man with a bunch of guys in uniform hoisting drinks. Him on a beach. Parachuting. Einstein kept panning the room as Seth grumbled about tiny screws and big thumbs. Bonnie almost looked away when she saw it.

"Stop the camera," Bonnie demanded.

Einstein fiddled with the buttons. "What did you see?"

"Back it up."

He rewound.

"There. Do you see it?"

Apparently he didn't because he shook his head.

"The ugly paperweight that looks like it was made by a six-year-old."

"What about it? Lots of guys bring mementos from their kids."

"But that's just it. This guy doesn't seem to have kids."

"And how do you figure that?"

"None of his pictures show him with a family. They're all images of a single guy, not a dad. I'll betcha that paperweight thing is a decoy."

"Seth, grab it, will you?"

"Sure thing." Pocketing the hard drive, which he'd finally popped free, Seth picked up the homemade-looking hunk and slid it into another pocket. "Anything else?"

"Nothing that really stands out. Take a look around, though. Maybe we missed something."

"There's a lot of blood in here," Seth observed. "Especially around his computer. Almost like someone died here."

"Maybe he did. Or was injured during the crash."

"Maybe."

Bonnie noted what Seth did, the copious amounts of black and reddish-brown fluid flooding the desk area. Perhaps the captain managed to stagger out into the hall in the hopes of finding aid. Judging by the large stain, she highly doubted he made it far.

A further search of the room, that involved the turning over of dirty clothing to Seth's disgust, didn't turn anything up and Seth left to join Astro in the command area. The other cyborg wasn't having an easy time, the room having sustained more damage than expected, but not from the crash.

"They shot the fucking place to hell so we couldn't get our hands on whatever it is they're hiding," Aramus growled, thumping his fist down on his armrest. "Bastards. We won't find anything useful there."

An avid watcher of conspiracy movies, Bonnie, however, saw a different scenario. "I don't think that's what happened. If you look at the blast marks and the way the bodies are positioned, it looks more like they were attacked."

"By their own crew?" Aramus couldn't hide the note of incredulity.

"It wouldn't be the first mutiny the military has suffered. It could also be a case of the ship went down and a soldier sensing their impending doom went a little nuts with his sidearm."

"Captain." Bolt's voice cut into their conjecture. "We've made it in to the engine room, but I don't think we're going to find anything useful. Looks like there was a massacre in here."

"Another suicidal soldier?" Aramus' skepticism rose another notch.

Or the same one. Bonnie gnawed her lower lip, the unfolding scene and evidence nagging at her. Given the extensive damage and loss of pressurization, not to mention oxygen, what human would have survived long enough to do that kind of damage? And again, why?

Flipping his screen to Bolt's camera frequency, Einstein rubbed his chin, his telltale tic for entering thinking mode. It seemed she wasn't the only one to jump to the conclusion they were dealing with a single entity. "The chances of two soldiers going rogue seem unlikely. Stay on high alert. We could have a possible hostile roaming."

"Bring it," Nova replied. "I'm more than willing to put down a rabid human."

Again, the sense of something not right nagged at her. *Why did they assume the killer and destroyer of the evidence was human? Most environmental suits can only carry a limited supply of oxygen. What if we are dealing with someone non human? Could the military ship have a cyborg aboard, an ally who seeks to help us?* Not wanting to sound foolish, she kept her non fact based theory to herself.

Einstein leaned in and stared intently at his screen, as if a closer view would show him what he wanted. "Bolt, do you see anything unusual about the energy core? Any equipment you're not familiar with?"

"Hard to tell with all the friggin' blast marks. Give me a second to clear some of the shit away." Bolt's gloved hands came into view, tugging at exposed wiring and bent metal. He grunted as he heaved a large chunk of fallen paneling away from the unit. "Huh. Will you look at this? Is that what you mean by strange-looking?" Bolt held up a small box with a single blinking green light, and Einstein let out a hissing breath.

"Shit." The expletive from Einstein sent a chill down her spine. "Bolt, put that thing down, nice and slow, then get the hell out of there. Quick. All of you evacuate the ship."

To his credit, Bolt did as he was told, but not without question. "What is it?"

"Bomb. And set on a short timer. Everyone needs to retreat and keep an eye open for a hostile. I'd say there's a ninety percent probability that you're not alone."

As a conversation stopper, it worked. Jaws dropped all over.

"But the life support is off. The ship depressurized. Human space suits aren't designed to last without an atmosphere for more than a few hours. No way is anyone still alive," Aramus blustered, his drumming fingers stilling.

"No one human, perhaps. But a cyborg could." Einstein spoke aloud what Bonnie, up until now, only suspected.

"A cyborg wouldn't hurt us," Nova huffed. "We're the good guys."

"A cyber unit still under military control might."

The suggestion put a grim expression on everyone's face. One human in a spacesuit, wandering around with a gun, was easily killed. A cyborg however? Now that could cause some serious damage.

On high alert, Bolt and Nova trotted down the hall and met up with Seth and Astro coming from the other direction. As a group, they made their way back into their small landing craft as Bonnie and the others watched and waited to see what, if anything would happen next.

It seemed almost anti-climatic when they managed to lift off without incident. Hell, they even cleared the downed military craft before it went up in a ball of dancing flames, the concussing waves barely rocking the small craft speeding away.

Aramus trusted the ease of their departure even less than her. "That was too easy. And I hate easy. Seth, scan the hull for trackers or unknown objects. Bolt and Astro, sweep the interior while Nova drives. I want every inch of the thing searched for possible intruders."

"You think we might have brought a castaway with us?" Seth asked, his steel knives tucked into his hands. As weapons went, it was a saner choice given in their cramped vessel. One stray blast could destabilize their spaceship and kill them all.

Einstein paused in his typing to answer. "I had a hand in designing the device Bolt found. Of course, when I left they were still in the testing phase. From what I recall, they have a short timer sequence, no more than fifteen minutes. Which means…"

"Someone set that bomb while we were on the ship."

"Unless the military adapted them since you last saw them."

"Possible," Einstein replied. "But unlikely. They were meant to be a suicide bomb. Once set, their main function was to go off quick before anyone could disarm them."

"Outer hull is clear," Seth announced.

"Engine compartment clear," Bolt added.

"Ditto for the rest of the ship," chimed in Astro.

The tension in the room eased. "Good. With any luck, whoever set the bomb died in the blast," Aramus said. "Still, though, just in case, I'm warning the onboard units to remain on high alert. Once the whole crew is assembled, we'll perform a ship wide sweep."

"I'm already running scans." Einstein's eyes remained riveted to his screen as his fingers flew fast enough to blur. "So far, I'm not detecting any exterior breaches, unknown accesses to our systems, or other anomalies."

"Keep looking. We don't want to bring any nasty surprises back with us. Joe will have my hide if I do."

As the cyborgs worked, Bonnie kept quiet. Her unease refused to dissipate even when the landing party returned, supposedly enemy free. She couldn't have said why or what bothered her. The repeated scans showed nothing strange or out of place. Everyone reported in safe and sound. They'd escaped and brought back the captain's hard drive, and the mysterious paperweight to boot.

So why did she chew her nails in a nervous habit her bionic status never managed to erase?

Why couldn't she relax?

Entering the command center, booty in hand, Seth proudly presented his treasures to Einstein. "Here you go, dude. All yours."

Einstein made a face. "Problem is, what should I do with it?"

"I thought the whole fucking point of the mission was intel. So crack the damned things and tell us what they say."

"I don't have a clean machine to work on them, though," Einstein replied with a frown. "If I hook them up to our ship's mainframe, I could inadvertently launch a malicious virus or tracking program."

"Then unhook a computer from the mainframe. You're the resident techno geek. Figure something out. Or were you bullshitting me when you said we needed this info pronto? What if there's important stuff on the drive, like plans for attack or worse?"

A sigh left Einstein. "I'm on it. I was just pointing out it won't be easy. I'll have to firewall my lab. In other words, cut off all access both wireless and wired to the rest of the ship, just in case."

"Then what are you waiting for? Get your metal ass moving."

"Do you need help?" Bonnie asked.

"I could use a hand just in case I come across some encrypted stuff. That's if you're up to it?"

She smiled. "I'm delighted to be of help."

"Oh make me gag." Aramus rolled his eyes. "Can we stick to the mission instead of turning this into a date? Both of you, get out of here and decode those devices. Let me know if you find anything."

"And he doesn't mean her sweet spot," Seth hollered as they exited. "Work before play."

"I know," Einstein grumbled.

She laced her fingers in his as they strode. "Come on, charming. Let's show your buddies what a great team we make and find something useful on these things. Then we can get to the playing."

"Sounds like a plan." He squeezed her fingers and for a moment, she could almost believe everything in the universe would turn out all right. Now if only she could dispel the sense that something overshadowed them waiting to swoop in and ruin the happiness she'd found.

Chapter Eighteen

As soon as he arrived at his workspace, Einstein sealed the room. He manually unhooked the cable that connected his computer to the rest of the ship and disabled the wireless aspect as well. Bonnie, perched on the metal counter of his workbench, legs dangling, watched.

"So what do you think we'll find on the drive?" she asked.

"A solution to peace between cyborgs and humans?"

She snorted. "Ha. Ha. You are turning into quite the comedian, charming."

A smile tilted his lips. "I keep trying. As to your question, in all honesty? Probably not much on the hard drive. I doubt the captain kept much of import on it."

"So why get Seth to grab it then?"

He rolled his shoulders. "You never know. If they were relying on a self destruct to destroy evidence then maybe they got sloppy. Could be the captain was the cocky sort as well, the kind who thinks nothing bad will ever happen to him."

"So you're going to check out the drive first? Why not the hunk of plaster?" Holding up the misshapen object, she squinted at it.

"Because I want to run tests on it first before cracking it open. I'd hate to take a hammer to the thing only to find out it has explosives inside." The look of horror on her face as she set it down carefully and scooted away made him snicker.

"You're fucking with me!" she exclaimed.

"Maybe a little. I highly doubt it's a bomb. But, I do want to be careful before slicing it open. I'd hate to damage the insides and render it useless. First, though, let's see what we can find on this."

Hooking up a mini power supply, Einstein managed to get the hard drive humming. "So far so good," he muttered. "Now where's that spare monitor I had in here?" Scrounging in a supply closet, he emerged with a flat screen and a handful of wires. He plopped them down beside her, then headed to a filing cabinet where he pulled out a green square with transistors and gold etchings all over it.

"Oh my God, where did you find that ancient motherboard?" she exclaimed, obviously recognizing the antiquated heap of plastic.

"The colonies we've visited over the years aren't exactly equipped with the best earth has to offer. Since I never know what might come in handy, I like to hold on to the stuff, just in case."

"Hoarder." She coughed the word in to her hand.

"I prefer the term collector of vintage artifacts."

She giggled. "I guess I shouldn't complain. Your need to collect useless objects is what led you to finding me."

"I'd hardly call you vintage. However, I'll admit, you're probably the most priceless item I've ever found."

He made a note that the compliment seemed to please her given her core temperature rose a few degrees. How fascinating. How distracting. He ignored his urge to explore it further. Right now, he needed to concentrate. With a little fiddling involving the attaching of ribbed cables and flicked dip switches on the old motherboard, he finally got things to work. His screen lit up as the impromptu computer system booted.

"I'm in," he announced.

"I wouldn't call a log in screen asking for a password in," Bonnie remarked, sliding off the counter so she could stand behind him, peering over his shoulder.

"Bah. Like that will stop me. You are talking to a master hacker." Cracking his fingers, a human gesture that came to him naturally even if he didn't recall doing it in his past life, he set to work.

With his knowledge and skills, it didn't take long for him to decipher the simple entry code and pull up all the files. Most he catalogued and ignored as they dealt with the boring, day to day details of running a ship—what broke, what needed fixing, who got reprimanded. Who cared?

What he was more interested in were the communications sent and received off ship. Those were hidden behind a few layers of security. Again, he didn't expect much, but it seemed in this case, he might be proven wrong. Several missives had bounced back and forth, encrypted of course. But before he could open them and look into them further, a file caught his attention. Bonnie spotted it the same moment he did, her finger stabbing at the screen and the video file dated to the time of the attack on the asteroid.

"What's in that one?"

"Let's find out."

The video began with a lot of static and noise, the wailing sound of a siren in the background strident, but not enough to hide the mumbled cursing of a man who plopped himself heavily in front of the camera. The blurred image of a star fleet uniform gave way to a visage, an ugly one. Heavy jowls, sunken eyes, and a receding hairline filled the screen.

"Fuck me, the camera is already running. Figures. Useless mechanical junk. Just another piece of crap that doesn't work like it's supposed to. Anyhow…to whoever gets this, if you get this, the ambush failed. Despite the new cloaking device, which someone assured me was foolproof, the cyborgs spotted us and managed to incapacitate our ships. Actually, they totally destroyed two and crashed ours. So much for sneaking up on them and taking them out." The human mopped at his sweaty face with a dirty towel. Tired, bloodshot eyes bored into theirs. "It's not looking fucking good. The bastards might not have been able to see us on radar, but that didn't prevent them from kicking our asses. The mission is an utter failure. We didn't capture any cybernetic specimens. Not even fucking close. Word from the asteroid is two were destroyed, but another four survived. Fuck, they kicked our ground troop's asses. It should be noted that the cyborgs have adapted to counter the Taser technology. My boys scored a few direct hits and while it seemed to freeze the cyber units for a few seconds, that was it. Once again, only direct headshots seem to incapacitate them. We do have some good news. We received confirmation that they are indeed in possession of cyborg unit B785. She is active and aiding the rebel cyborgs. Attempts to regain control of her have failed. She has not succumbed to any of the override codes." The captain sighed. "And now you're up to date. At this point, we've lost. I've initialized the self destruct sequence for this vessel; however, the power is failing rapidly so God only knows if it will go off in time. Hell, I don't even know if we have enough power to send this message off. I'm heading for the life pods as soon as I send this. Just in case we don't manage to destroy the craft, we're manually wiping the hard drives as I record this. I don't know who the fuck's brilliant idea it was to confront these bastards but whoever you are, you're a fucking idiot. Court martial me if you like, but it's the truth. I don't care what technology we have, those bastards are smart. And deadly. Here's to hoping someone picks me up at the rendezvous point. If not, we're all dead men."

A thick finger stabbed at the keyboard out of sight, but must have missed because the camera kept recording. A flask came up and the captain took a less than healthy swig. The sirens suddenly cut out and an eerie silence descended, broken only by the captain's breathing. A swish of the door opening saw the captain turning his head. He half rose from his seat. "What is it? Why are you here instead of heading for the pods? What—" A gurgle sounded and the body slumped back, onto the screen. A moment later, the video stopped.

Stunned, Einstein took a moment to absorb it.

"That's it?" Bonnie asked.

"Yes."

"I'd say it's safe to say he didn't manage to send the message."

"No. Looks like he died, which means the military might not know what's happened yet."

"You mean someone killed him."

So it appeared. But who?

Bonnie voiced his question aloud. "Someone intentionally killed the captain, and then dragged his body out of sight. Why hide the body?"

"So we wouldn't suspect there was a mutiny?"

She shook her head. "That makes no sense. Elsewhere they didn't bother to hide the evidence. Someone wanted us to see that video."

"But we didn't learn much."

"Didn't we? We learned that they do have new technology."

"Which we already knew about."

"That they were tracking us before we hit the asteroid."

"Which we suspected, given the ambush."

"And that there's a spy onboard with us."

So she'd caught the subtle reference too. But did she realize the implication? The spy most likely came in the form of their newest member— Bonnie.

No. Einstein didn't want to believe it. Something in his expression must have given him away because her lips tightened. "And no, before you even go there, it's not me. Or weren't you paying attention? The way the captain worded the message, he spoke as if someone else confirmed my existence and reactivation. That means someone on this ship is working for the military!"

"Impossible. I've known these cyborgs for years. They wouldn't betray—"

The door to his lab opened, despite the security lock, and Astro appeared in the opening.

Einstein frowned. "What is it? You're not supposed to be here…" He trailed off, noting the gun in the cyborg's hand, a gun aimed at him. "Oh, Astro, don't tell me you're working for the humans?" Astro was the spy? But how? Einstein had cleaned out his BCI himself. He'd have vouched on his life Astro didn't have any remaining military taint or programming. Unless someone got to him… But how? When?

207

For some reason, a flash of their most recent stop at the bordello popped up. Einstein wanted to groan. *We're all fucking idiots.* They'd worried so much about their vessel getting tracked, they never thought to check themselves. Einstein wanted to hang his head in shame. However, recriminations would have to wait. Death stared him and Bonnie in the face. He didn't need to calculate their odds to know they weren't good. "Why?" he whispered. After all they'd been through. Why turn on his brethren?

"I had to."

"Had to?" Einstein couldn't hide the note of incredulity. "That makes no sense. You had your freedom."

"But they had my brother. He came to see me when we were visiting the bordello."

"Why didn't you tell me?"

"I couldn't."

Couldn't or wouldn't? Did it matter? "Came to see you and what?"

"None of your business. Suffice it to say, he made me see things in a different light."

"I'll bet he did." Probably via some virus he transmitted to Astro. "Where is your brother now?"

"He was on the other ship," Bonnie concluded in a quiet voice that drew Astro's gaze for just a second.

"He was."

Einstein noted the past tense, but ignored it to ask. "How much did you tell them? How much did you compromise us?"

"Not much. I knew if I didn't hold information back, they'd just kill us both."

"But you told them where we were going."

"Yes. And about B785. Enough to keep them happy."

"Did Ralph and Fred really die in the ambush, or was that your doing too?"

By his very silence, Astro damned himself.

Anger flooded Einstein's synapses. "What about our homeworld? Did you betray everyone there too?"

"No. They're safe for now." A ghost of a smile twisted Astro's lip. "Good job locking that information down. Even though I tried, I couldn't give it away."

A small sense of relief flooded Einstein. As a precautionary measure, only a small handful of cyborgs knew the actual coordinates of the cyborg planet. Einstein programmed the units that way. In case of capture, it meant the military couldn't just retrieve the information and mount an invasion. Thank their nano technology for that foresight. But their biggest secret kept safe didn't let Astro off the hook.

"You should have told me about your brother. We could have saved him."

"And risk your precious female?" The threatening cyborg sneered. A bitter laugh escaped Astro. "Just like you were all willing to do anything to keep her safe, so am I to rescue my brother. See, if I don't do what they say, they'll detonate the bomb they've got inside him. I can't let that happen."

"So you'd let the safety of one trump that of hundreds?"

"He's my brother. I might not remember a lot of things about my humanity, but I do remember one thing. Family sticks together. I'm sorry, Einstein. I really did like you and the others, but…" Astro shrugged. "I promised my parents I'd take care of him."

Cursing the fact he'd firewalled his lab too well in the hopes of containing any possible viruses, Einstein frantically tried to think a way out of their dilemma. Unarmed, with only his wits, things didn't look good, but he wouldn't let bad odds prevent him from doing the right thing. As he saw Astro's finger pressing on the trigger, Einstein lunged, but a small body threw him off balance as Bonnie darted in front of him. He heard her gasp of pain as she took the shot meant for him. To the floor she crumpled in a dead heap.

"Bonnie! No!" Seeing red, his rage overwhelming his cortex, Einstein dove with only his bare hands as his weapon at the treacherous cyborg who dared to hurt the one thing that made him feel alive. Before Astro could fire again, they went down in a tangle of limbs, clawing and wrestling, their bodies too tightly entwined to land any blows of consequence. The gun went skittering across the floor as Einstein managed to grasp the hand holding it and slammed it a few times.

Weaponless, Astro nevertheless snarled. "Idiot. Don't you know it's too late? Even now, my brother is destroying the engines. Killing the others. Join us. We don't have to fight anymore. The military will take us back. Leave us our memories so long as we aid them in bringing in the others. We could live without looking over our shoulders all the time. They've even promised us access to our families."

Bonnie said it more eloquently than he ever could have.

"Like fuck," she growled before pressing the muzzle of the rescued gun against Astro's head and pulling the trigger. One loud explosion and the body under him went limp. Cyborgs could heal from a lot of things, but direct head shots, especially ones at close range, weren't one of them.

Einstein rolled off the corpse and jumped to his feet, his concern immediately flashing to Bonnie. "Show me your injury. We need to stem the blood flow and assess the damage."

"Chill, charming. It's only a scratch. I was playing dead."

His robotic eyes roved her frame, noting the shallow furrow along her arm instead of the gigantic hole he'd imagined. "Played? Why?"

She smirked at him. "Because I thought you'd enjoy a chance to slay the dragon and save the princess."

"Some slaying. You killed him, not me."

"Yeah, well, you were taking too long. But don't worry, up until the part where you let him talk, you were kicking some serious ass. Did I mention how hot you were while doing it? Like, seriously hot. You can come to my rescue anytime. However, next time, do it shirtless, would you?" She winked.

He actually growled before yanking her close to him. "You brat! Don't you ever scare me like that again." He shook her.

Up came her hands to cup his cheeks. "Sorry, charming. I can't promise that. Now, my turn to ask, are you alright?"

"I sustained no real injury."

"I wasn't talking about that. I mean, I just killed one of your buddies. Are you okay with that? Are you traumatized? Sad?"

"He was a traitor."

"He was also your friend."

In this case, cold logic countered any emotion he might have had. Einstein's gaze hardened. "A true friend wouldn't have killed fellow cyborgs and would have trusted me to help him and his brother."

"Speaking of whom, he spoke like his brother was onboard. We need to warn the others."

"The communications in this room are disabled. We need to leave the room and get to an active communication console."

Before they could act, a pounding erupted at the door, which had slid shut after Astro's entry and relocked itself. Einstein strode over and yanked the portal open, cursing as he fumbled with the manual controls. Seth rushed in, his usually pristine coif mussed. "Dude, you'll never believe this but some guy, a cyborg who looks just like Astro, but one that we never liberated, tried to kill Nova and Bolt and take out our engine room."

"Oh, I believe it."

"You mean you knew? Did you crack the hard drive already? Did…" Seth's voice trailed off as he took in the carnage on the floor. "Shit. I see you found out the hard way. You both okay?"

"Nothing a shower and some therapy won't fix."

"Therapy?" Bonnie's brow arched. "I thought you said you were okay?"

"Physically, but mentally, I think I need some healing."

Immediately, her face creased in concern. "What can I do to help?"

"Get the shower going."

"How is that supposed to help?"

Seth laughed. "Oh, princess. I think you've created a monster. Brainiac here needs some sexual healing, which means I should get out of here."

"Take that with you." Einstein pointed to the body. "And eject it along with his brother's body. I'd suggest doing it quickly. Apparently, the military claimed Astro's brother had a bomb inside him. Seeing as how our ship is still intact, I'm going to assume death doesn't trigger it, but let's not take any chances."

"A bomb? Shit! And what will you be doing while I risk blowing up some crucial part of my anatomy?"

"Getting that sexual healing you were just talking about."

"Now isn't the time," Bonnie said primly.

"Oh yes it is."

For once, Seth was thinking with his head instead of his dick. "She's right. It isn't. We should report to Aramus."

"You can do that right after you flush the bodies. Now, Seth," Einstein replied in a firm tone. "Or do you want to see what subroutine I've got programmed in your BCI?" He didn't have one, but Seth didn't know that.

Ignoring Seth's grumble about bossy intelligence bots with too much pent up testosterone, Einstein advanced on Bonnie.

She licked her lips. "We really should go see the boss."

"After we clean up."

"What you have in mind isn't clean, charming."

"Oh, I beg to differ. I find it most *cleansing*." He purred the last word and smiled as her breathing hitched. With a squeal, she turned and dashed into the bathroom, him on her heels.

Duty might be the cyborg way, but Einstein was more than a robot. And he had needs. Needs that required tending. Now.

Covered in the fleshly matter of a fallen former friend should have killed his ardor, but his relief at discovering Bonnie unscathed trumped everything. Well, almost everything. He still felt a great need to reassure himself she was alive. That he was alive. And despite what duty demanded, he'd take care of that need first. He'd allow himself to be selfish because he was more than a cyborg or a machine. He was first and foremost a man. A horny man with a naked woman—who he loved more than anything—waiting for him under a warm spray with a beckoning smile.

It took only a few seconds for him to shred the clothes from his body and join her. Turned to face the wall of the shower, Bonnie smiled coyly at him over her shoulder. He pressed against her slick back, his cock rubbing along the crease of her ass, her head turned so their lips could fuse together.

"I thought I'd lost you," he whispered between licks and nips, the horror of the moment still fresh in his memory.

"We won," she murmured back. "Just like in the fairytales, good triumphed over evil."

"Your stories forgot to mention the fact the hero almost dies of a heart attack in the process."

She chuckled. "Oh please. You have a biomechanical heart and I have healing nanobots. Besides, it would take more than one bullet to kill our love."

Einstein groaned.

"Too much?" she teased.

"Yes. But I've got the cure for corny one-liners." Parting her wet thighs, he probed her sex with the tip of his cock. She pushed back against

215

him, tilting her hips to take more than just the head of him into her. He obliged, sheathing his length in her channel, feeling every atom in his body come alive.

"Mmm," she hummed. "If this is how every battle ends, then remind me to not miss a mission."

In he thrust, hard enough to make her gasp. "Oh no you don't. I'm going to lock you in a castle where you're safe, princess."

She scrabbled at the wet walls as he pounded into her. "You'd better plan on staying with me then because I won't stay behind while you go facing danger."

"I don't plan on ever leaving your side."

Her brilliant green eyes met his in a stare that wrenched his entire being. "Promise?"

"Bonnie, I love you. You make me feel alive. You make me want to live. You make me a better man. One who is more than just a sum of parts. Just try and get rid of me."

"Oh, charming." She sighed his nickname. "For a cyborg who claimed once upon a time that he had no emotions, or a single clue, you say the most beautiful things. Now less talk and more fuck. Princess wants to come."

Laughter, a natural sound he'd once thought himself incapable of, slipped from his lips, and soon changed to panting. And to think he'd once thought passion was just a thing made up of hormones. Good thing he found the right woman to teach him better.

*

It took a second round of lovemaking before Einstein declared himself recovered enough to meet with the rest of the crew. To her surprise, no one said a thing when they finally showed up, although Seth did have to hide a knowing smirk.

Given the treachery of Astro, she expected a somber pall, but she'd not counted on the cyborg way of handling things. In their minds, things were very black and white. Astro had a choice. He could have asked for help. He would have even gotten it. Instead, he betrayed them. And for that, no one had any sympathy.

The bodies of the traitors were ejected into space and ashed with the onboard lasers. Aramus didn't want to leave any evidence of them behind, most especially their cortexes. That wasn't the only thing that occurred while she and Einstein took care of business. An emergency message was sent to the cyborg homeworld detailing the events. Joe and the others needed to know there was a possibility their location was compromised and take extra measures to keep everyone safe. Einstein, however, didn't seem at all concerned, his faith in his programming of the units unshaken despite the fact the military managed to get so close to one of his friends.

As for the hard drive, they didn't find anything else of interest on it, the final recording the only thing of value or interest. Aramus was less than impressed.

And as for the paperweight?

Paper Mache and paint. As it turned out, it was a gift from the captain's niece. If the captain hid any secrets, they blew up when the ship did. In the end, they were no further ahead even if Aramus and the others counted their results after the military's ambush attempt at a victory.

Bonnie reserved judgment. She knew all too well the dragon, and despite this setback, she doubted General Doom would give up, but at the same time, she wouldn't worry about it. She'd been given a precious gift. The gift of a second chance. A chance for a fairy tale ending with her prince charming, and dammit, she planned to enjoy every second of it.

Because I am more than a machine. More than a tool for the military. I am Bonnie. Flawed princess, enhanced human, and cherished lover of the most wonderful man in the universe. Despite what the future might bring, she had everything to live for. And best of all? She was loved.

As for the humans who thought to take it away?

Bring it, you bastards. Because I intend to fight for my right to love and happiness. I won't let anyone, and I mean anyone, take away my happily ever after without a fight. Even if it meant disobeying Einstein about staying out of the path of danger. Besides, she loved his idea of *punishment*. It was why she programmed Aramus' chair to do that very naughty thing. It was worth every single chastising moment of his lashing tongue.

Epilogue

It took forever to reach the cyborg homeworld, long enough for Bonnie to just about drain him. Despite the research Einstein had done on human females and their emotional reactions, his girlfriend—as she liked to call herself—didn't react to stress in conventional methods. She didn't rely on food, exercise, or displays of emotional drama. No, his female was unique in that she used sex as a catharsis. Not that he truly minded. His stamina could more than keep up with her sexual appetite; it was the teasing he put up with that grew tiresome. Although, Einstein did secretly enjoy Seth's jealousy.

"Could you keep it down a little at night?" Seth groused on more than one occasion.

Coached by his girlfriend, Einstein leaned back in his seat and tossed him a lazy smile. "Jealous?"

"Fucking right, I am. Not all of us are lucky enough to have a woman to call our own. And I'm mighty tired of tugging one with my ten friends." Seth waggled his fingers and Einstein laughed.

"Let me see, what would you say if you were in my shoes?" Einstein tapped his chin. "Oh yeah. Too bad, so sad, suck-ah!"

The slang coming from his lips made Seth stare at him for a stunned moment before they both broke into big gales of laughter. It was a laughter Bonnie shared with him when he relayed the conversation to her as they waited to dock. With a thud, the ship hit solid ground and her mirth died. She clenched his hand tight, so tight his nanobots rushed to the area to repair the damage, but he didn't say a word. He knew how she looked forward to and dreaded this moment. Unfortunately, given communication was reserved for emergencies only, she'd not gotten much of a chance to converse with her sister. For some reason, the idea of meeting with her sibling both exhilarated and terrified her.

"I think I'm going to throw up," Bonnie said as she gulped unnecessary air.

"You are not ill, nor are we performing maneuvers."

"Yeah, and yet my stomach is churning and my nerves are shot."

"If you do vomit, try to keep it to the side. I just shined my boots."

The dirty look she directed his way made him chuckle, but she eased up a bit on her grip. "I think I liked you better when you didn't get my jokes."

"Truly?"

"No. I love you, Einstein."

"And I love you too, princess." Yes, he'd finally caved and started calling her by the nickname most of the crew adopted. It seemed apt.

After all, they'd met under extraordinary circumstances, fallen in love freeing him from the shackles which hid his humanity, vanquished everything in their path, and found passion in each other's arms. Now they just needed to live their happily ever after. Or would as soon as they completed this one last step.

The rumble of the engines died as they powered down. The interior pressurized and the bay doors slid open. Bright sunlight streamed in along with foliage scented air, a refreshing change from the recycled gases on the ship. A gangplank extended from the vessel. Bonnie, despite the fact she didn't need to breathe, practically hyperventilated.

"Ready?" he asked softly.

"No." She laughed nervously. "Silly, huh? Here I've been dying to see my sister and now I'm scared and wishing we were back in space."

"Never silly. Just nervous, which my studies say is normal."

"You and your studies," she scoffed, yet her grip on him loosened an iota.

Together, they strode into the sunshine, fingers laced, but not for long.

A squealed, "Bonnie!" tore his girlfriend from his side as she ran to meet the dashing figure of Chloe, who couldn't wait a moment longer to reunite.

The pair made a touching sight even to cyborgs hardened by circumstance and programming. Aramus, ever the diplomatic one, managed an only slightly sarcastic, "Get a room," as he skirted the hugging sisters.

Standing to the side, Joe gazed fondly upon the reunited sisters, a hint of moisture in his eyes. "Thanks for bringing her home," he said softly as Einstein came up beside him.

"Don't thank me. Thank fate or whatever magic brought me to her in the first place."

"Holy shit. Don't tell me you don't have a logical explanation for what happened?"

"Nope. It appears not everything in the universe has a scientific answer." Some things just happened. And while happiness couldn't be predicted or created or dissected into parts, Einstein still appreciated the end result.

He might have started out his mission as a cyborg who thought science and logic were the only things that mattered, but he returned home realizing that some things just didn't have an explanation. Love happened. Fairy tales could exist, even for cyborgs. Anyone could have their happily ever after.

Even a geeky prince charming and a bionic princess.

*

Where's a damned bar when you need one? Heading toward the forest that always calmed him, Seth left the love fest behind before anyone saw the tears or heard him sniffle. Sometimes, his human side was all too strong. All too envious.

He wished his buddy Einstein well, he truly did. Him and all the other cyborgs who had discovered love and something to make their lives worth living. But at times, he wished, weak as it made him sound, that he could also find the same kind of joy, and acceptance.

Maybe one day my turn will come.

Of course, he didn't expect it to happen so quickly.

He froze as the muzzle of a pistol nestled against the back of his head. Then smiled at the tickle of a familiar scent. "Well hello there, darling. I knew you couldn't resist me forever."

"I see you're still just as annoying."

Whirling, Seth held his hands up so the gun pointed at his forehead. He came face to face with the lady who haunted his dreams. His ex-partner. The only woman he'd ever loved. The only one who ever spurned him. The woman he'd once called wife.

The End

More Books by Eve Langlais

Published by Amira Press:
Alien Mate, Alien Mate 2, Alien Mate 3
Broomstick Breakdown
Dating Cupid
Pack Series: Defying Pack Law, Betraying The Pack, Seeking Pack Redemption
Taming Her Wolf
His Teddy Bear
Scared of Spiders
The Hunter (Realm series)

Published by Liquid Silver Books:
Princess of Hell series: Lucifer's Daughter, Snowballs In Hell, Hell's Revenge
Crazy
Date With Death
Hybrid Misfit
Last Minion Standing
Toxic
Wickedest Witch

Published by Eve Langlais
The Geek Job
Furry United Coalition: Bunny And The Bear, Swan And The Bear, Croc And The Fox
Freakn' Shifters: Delicate Freakn' Flower, Jealous And Freakn', Already Freakn' Mated
Alien Abduction: Accidental Abduction, Intentional Abduction, Dual Abduction
Cyborgs: More Than Machines: C791, F814
Welcome To Hell: A Demon And His Witch, A Demon And His Psycho

Author Biography

Hello and thanks for taking the time to read something I wrote. I do hope I managed to entertain you – and make you giggle a time or two. Since you're actually checking out this note, I guess it means you're curious about me, so here's the scoop.

I am a mom of three, who is just shy of forty. I am married (over thirteen years now) to a man whom I adore – when he's not driving me insane. A true romantic, I totally believe in love at first sight. But then again, I also think there is life 'out' there – hopefully as sexy as the aliens I've created in my mind. Lol.

I am Canadian, but being a military brat, I've been coast to coast. Right now, I'm living in the Ottawa area – hockey, poutine and beavertails, yay – and enjoying the chaos of family life.

If you want to know more about me, then I guess I should mention you can visit me at

http://www.EveLanglais.com

Sexy covers, excerpts, my blog, and other items that might interest you, await. Be sure to sign up for my new release mailing list if you'd like to know when my next story will be available for your reading enjoyment.

Until we meet in the pages of a book again, wishing you tons of great reading and smiles,

Eve

3271851R00120

Printed in Great Britain
by Amazon.co.uk, Ltd.,
Marston Gate.